"I made it thro
your bones an

Trevor's startled laughter was loud in the quiet dining room.

Olivia stared at him, shocked at herself. "I did *not* say that. Some alien took over my body and made those words come out of my mouth."

"Or maybe you've tuned into my impulsive behavior."

"I don't think it works that way."

"Who knows? It might." Heat flickered in his gaze. "It's not easy making polite conversation while I'm calculating the weight-bearing capabilities of this table."

"Why would you do that?"

"Just trying to decide if it would hold us both."

"Trevor!" She pressed her hands to her cheeks.

"You didn't think of it?"

"*No.*"

"Not even once?"

"Of course not! I've never—" She stopped herself, but it was too late.

His expression softened. "Nothing wrong with that."

A COWBOY'S COURAGE

THE MCGAVIN BROTHERS

Vicki Lewis Thompson

Ocean Dance Press

A COWBOY'S COURAGE
© 2017 Vicki Lewis Thompson

ISBN: 978-1-946759-19-1

Ocean Dance Press LLC
PO Box 69901
Oro Valley, AZ 85737

Cover art by Kristin Bryant

Visit the author's website at
VickiLewisThompson.com

Want more cowboys? Check out these other titles by Vicki Lewis Thompson

The McGavin Brothers
A Cowboy's Strength
A Cowboy's Honor
A Cowboy's Return
A Cowboy's Heart
A Cowboy's Courage

Thunder Mountain Brotherhood
Midnight Thunder
Thunderstruck
Rolling Like Thunder
A Cowboy Under the Mistletoe
Cowboy All Night
Cowboy After Dark
Cowboy Untamed
Cowboy Unwrapped
In the Cowboy's Arms
Say Yes to the Cowboy
Do You Take This Cowboy?

Sons of Chance
Wanted!
Ambushed!
Claimed!
Should've Been a Cowboy
Cowboy Up
Cowboys Like Us
Long Road Home
Lead Me Home
Feels Like Home
I Cross My Heart

_1_

Trevor McGavin parked his truck in front of what used to be the Campbell house but now belonged to Olivia Shaw. The outside looked about the way he remembered it from years ago. The screened-in front porch had been freshly painted but it was the same shade of brown.

Grabbing a carton of eggs from the passenger seat, he climbed out and walked through a patch of wild grass that crunched under his boots. Out of habit he pushed back his hat and glanced up. Not a cloud in sight. Damn.

Southwestern Montana desperately needed rain, but the October sky was an unrelenting blue. As a backdrop for red, yellow and orange leaves, it was a stunner. A hard downpour would end that display, but Trevor had spent the past two months training as a volunteer with the Eagles Nest Fire Department. He and his buddies at the station would gladly trade fall color for a gully washer.

He took the cement walk to the porch. The hinges on the screen door squeaked. As a kid, he hadn't noticed things like that. Now he had the urge to grab a can of WD-40 and fix it.

He almost expected to see toy trucks strewn around. He and Bryce had gone to school with Jeremy Campbell and they'd spent a good bit of time out on the porch playing with their trucks. The redwood furniture was the same but the cushions were different.

Olivia must have heard him coming because she opened the front door before he could knock. "You brought eggs from Kendra!"

He tugged on the brim of his hat. "Yes, ma'am."

"On top of you fixing my drywall, too. That's above and beyond. Thank you, Trevor."

"Mom's enamored of those chickens. She feels obliged to spread the wealth."

"I appreciate it." She took the eggs and ushered him inside. "Fresh eggs are a luxury."

"That's what Mom says." Olivia looked different, although she had on her glasses and wore her long, dark hair pulled back with a clip like he normally saw it.

But whenever she came to Wild Creek Ranch she dressed in a blouse and skirt that made her appear businesslike. Then again, accountants were supposed to project that image, right? Otherwise people wouldn't trust them to sort out their finances.

Evidently when Olivia was off-duty she preferred jeans and a sweater. The moss-colored knit fabric draped her breasts in a way he shouldn't be noticing. Besides being the McGavin family accountant, she was the least flirtatious woman he'd ever met.

His mom believed it was because she'd lost her soulmate. Although it had been three years since Edward's death, she likely wasn't over it and might never be. Trevor had met the guy a few times and had liked him. Ogling his widow when she showed zero interest was just wrong.

Better to focus on the house. The outside might look the same, but the inside sure didn't. Before the dominant color had been beige. That had been replaced with bright colors and lots of plants. The place even smelled different, like citrus.

He glanced around. "Are you burning a scented candle?" After his firefighting training, he was less tolerant of lit candles.

"It's a diffuser." She pointed to where it sat on a side table.

He grinned. "Let me guess. You bought one after getting a massage from April."

"I did."

"I swear half the town is diffusing essential oils these days thanks to her. Not that I object. They're safer than candles."

"That's what I decided."

"I just think it's funny that everywhere I go, there's a diffuser."

"I love mine. Let me put the eggs in the fridge and then I'll show you the wall."

"Sure. No rush. I don't have anything else going on this afternoon."

"And lucky you," she called over her shoulder as she went into the kitchen, "you get to do a maintenance chore for me instead of relaxing with a beer."

"Happy to do it." Until recently he and his brothers had used any spare time to work on the second barn at Wild Creek Ranch, but that was finished. Between firehouse duty, his job with Paladin Construction and the barn project, his days had been packed.

He'd joked with his mom that he didn't know what to do with a free Saturday afternoon. She'd promptly sent him over to repair Olivia's wall. That would teach him.

But it was okay. Olivia was always looking for ways to keep the ranch from paying too much in taxes. His mom adored her.

"I hope this won't take too much of your time." She reappeared and started down the hall. "The hole's not very big. It's in my bedroom."

As he followed her, he glanced into the room that used to be Jeremy's. It was an office now. The house seemed a lot smaller than it had when he was a kid. "Didn't there used to be three bedrooms?"

"There were. We took out the wall between the third one and the master so we could have a master suite. Did you know the Campbells?"

"Bryce and I are the same age as their son. We used to hang out with him."

"They seem like nice people."

"Yes, ma'am."

"You have beautiful cowboy manners, Trevor, but the way you call me *ma'am* makes me feel ancient."

"Sorry, I just—"

"I know. Kendra taught all her boys to be polite. I love that." She walked into the room and turned to face him. "But how about calling me Olivia?"

Simple request. But it knocked him off kilter and gave him ideas he likely shouldn't be entertaining. "I can do that."

"Thank you." She pointed to an inside wall. "The damage is over there."

"Huh." He crossed to a hole that could have been made by a short guy putting his fist through it. He'd bet the keys to his work truck that wasn't the explanation. "If you don't mind my asking, how did this happen?"

"I kicked it."

Dumbfounded, he turned to her. "While you were doing what, exactly?"

"Practicing my kickboxing."

"Kickboxing."

"It's great exercise."

That would explain how toned she looked under the jeans and sweater. "I've never seen it done so I'll take your word for it. They teach kickboxing classes somewhere in Eagles Nest?"

"No. I drive to Bozeman once a week and practice at home in between lessons. I was really into it one night and I misjudged how close I was to the wall."

"Did you hurt your foot?"

"Fortunately not. I was wearing running shoes with a thick sole."

"That's good." He would love her to recreate the scene for him but figured asking was inappropriate. "Is it anything like karate?"

"Somewhat."

"Then it's probably good for self-defense."

"It could be, I guess."

"Then I can see why you'd want to learn something like that since you live alone."

She smiled. "This is Eagles Nest. One of the reasons Edward and I moved here was the incredibly low crime rate. For two people born and raised in Chicago, it was a big selling point."

"So you only do it for exercise?" He wasn't buying it.

"Well, that and for…anger management."

"Seriously?" He nudged back his hat. "I can't imagine you needing such a thing."

"Me, either, which is why I didn't recognize an emotion like rage. It was so unlike me. Then one night in the kitchen I started screaming and smashing dishes."

"I'm having so much trouble picturing this. You're—"

"Quiet? Reserved?"

"Exactly."

"I used to be very quiet, but after Edward died my outward calm was an act. Inwardly I was furious. It wasn't fair. I was mad at him, mad at the world, mad at the doctors who'd failed to save him."

He nodded. "Yeah, that makes sense. It wasn't fair. He was too young."

"Exactly. Kendra's the only person I ever told about my meltdown and she suggested I start doing something physical, preferably where I'd get to pound on things. Kickboxing lets me do that."

He glanced at the hole in the wall. "Are you still angry?"

"No, thank goodness. The kickboxing worked great and once I faced what was wrong with me, I got some counseling. This truly was an accident. I didn't go into a rage and kick the wall in."

"Good to know."

"How long will it take to fix it?"

"Not long. Less than an hour. I'll get my stuff from the truck."

"I told Kendra I'd pay you."

He shook his head. "No, ma—" He cleared his throat. "No, Olivia." He liked saying her name. It wasn't one he came across every day. "I'm grateful for the outstanding job you do for Mom and the ranch."

"She pays me for that so I should pay you for this."

"Still not taking it. Be right back." He touched the brim of his hat and left the room.

Whew. Olivia was *nothing* like the cool, collected accountant he'd pegged her as. Smashing dishes. Kickboxing. His mom could have warned him.

But no, she wouldn't have. His mom had received that information in confidence. He wouldn't go blabbing it, either, and he was kind of flattered that Olivia had entrusted him with it.

Then again, she had a hole in her wall and she might have decided telling the truth about it was her best option. She wouldn't have had to add the part about anger management, though. Or smashing dishes because she was furious that her young husband had up and died on her.

But she'd been open with him and he was more motivated than ever to give her a nice repair job. After strapping on his tool belt and hauling his toolbox out of the truck, he loaded his other supplies into a plastic tote and carried both back to the house.

She was at the door and held it for him. "I really appreciate this. I've looked at that stupid hole for two weeks and it bothers me. The rest of the room is beautiful, but the hole just ruins it."

"It'll be gone as of today." He followed her down the hall. This time he was more aware that they were headed into her bedroom. Before he'd been too distracted by their conversation to take much note of the space other than the damaged wall. Did she have a picture of her late husband on a nightstand? He'd look.

"I got out the paint just now, but I'll handle that after you've finished the patch. It probably has to dry for a while."

"Not as much as you might think. I brought a fast-working compound and if you have a hair dryer, we can get the whole thing done, paint and all."

"With all this hair, you know I have a hair dryer."

Now that she'd mentioned it, he paid more attention to the luxurious hair captured by a silver clip. It hung in glossy waves nearly to her waist and rippled with each step she took. Hair that long took a while to grow. Three years?

A paint can and brush sat beside the wall. "Lucky you still have the same batch."

"I was pretty sure I did. I repainted about six months ago when I redecorated the bedroom."

"Ah." That made the project less creepy. He shouldn't care if the room looked the way it had when she'd shared it with her late husband. But he was more willing to admire the color scheme if it was new.

Setting down his toolbox and his materials on the hardwood floor, he took a quick look around. The walls were a warm pink that picked up the dominant color in a large abstract piece of artwork hanging over the bed.

He'd never understood pictures that didn't look like anything specific, but this one drew him in for some reason. For want of a better word, he'd say it was arousing. The curtains and bedding were ivory, and she'd added some throw pillows to the bed in various shades of pink. No picture of Edward anywhere.

He turned to her. "You did a great job."

"It's super girly."

"I wouldn't say that. I think of girly as ruffles and lace everywhere. I'd call this womanly."

"Hm." She glanced around. "I like that."

"I forgot a drop cloth to protect your floor. I have one in the truck." He started out the door.

"Never mind. I have one you can use. I'll get it."

"Thanks." After she left he crouched down to see if the paint color had a name. Most of them did these days and this shade was unfamiliar to him. Turned out it was called Eros.

Standing, he gazed at the shades of pink in the picture hanging over the bed. Even though abstract art didn't have to represent anything, maybe the artist had been thinking of a flower. A rose.

He studied the pink swirls. Not a rose. Damned if the soft-focus pattern didn't remind him of a very special place on a woman's body, one of his favorites. Okay, he was just going there because of the name on the paint can.

Olivia came back with the drop cloth, and he whirled away from his close examination as if he'd been caught doing something he shouldn't.

She handed him the drop cloth. "Do you like abstract art?"

"Not usually. But I like that."

"Me, too. I was drawn to it even though normally I'm into primary colors. Once I bought it to go over the bed, I went a little pink crazy."

"Interesting name for your paint."

"Isn't it?" Her cheeks flushed. "I wanted to bring out the color in the artwork and then it had that hokey name. I took the paint and ignored the name."

"Just a marketing gimmick."

"I know, right?" She hesitated. "Anything I can do to help?"

"Just keep me company."

"Sure thing." She sat on the edge of the bed.

God help him, he took his time with that repair. He could have been finished in under an hour, but he dragged it out from the estimated one hour to two. She didn't call him on it, either.

Instead she kept him company as he'd requested. She wanted to hear about the six months he and his twin Bryce had spent in Texas working cattle. He surprised himself by telling stories that he'd never bothered to share with anyone.

When he got tired of talking about himself, he asked her what it was like growing up in Chicago. She mentioned the cultural things— museums, art galleries, live theater. But it turned out she didn't miss them enough to move back there. Eagles Nest was her home, now.

Their conversation was outwardly casual and friendly. Yet the entire time he battled sexual tension. He blamed the picture and being alone in a bedroom with the fascinating woman who'd bought it. He had no idea if she had a similar reaction to him. Repairing the wall required him to keep his back to her and he couldn't read her expression.

While he used her hair dryer on the patch, they couldn't talk at all. She stayed on the bed, though, and had to be watching him. His body heated up right along with that patch.

Eventually he sanded the patch, applied two coats of Eros and the job was done. He began packing up. "That should do it."

"The wall looks great. I can't thank you enough."

"You're welcome." He glanced at her. Was that a gleam of interest in her eyes? Or was it a reflection from her glasses? Wishful thinking could get a guy in trouble.

"Could I at least offer you a beer?"

He was so damned tempted, but when he relaxed with a beer he tended to let down his guard. He might say the wrong thing and ruin whatever might or might not be developing. "Thanks, but I'd better take a raincheck. I promised Bryce I'd stop by the Guzzling Grizzly on my way home and he probably wonders where I am."

"Goodness, it's later than I thought. Time flies when you're repairing a wall."

"I took a little extra care." He surveyed the room. "You did a great job in here and I wanted to make sure the patch blended."

"Which it completely does."

"I have to ask, though, do you have any idea if that painting is supposed to represent something?"

"Not that I know of. Hang on. I might have the name." She crossed to her bedside table, opened the drawer and took out a small white card. Then she blushed. "I'd forgotten this. It's called *La Séduction.*"

"Hm." He'd never learned French but he had no trouble translating.

Her blush deepened. "Honestly, the name had nothing to do with it. I just loved the colors."

"They're good colors." He fantasized walking over there and drawing her gently into his arms. Then he'd kiss those cheeks that were the same pink as her walls. Instead he grabbed his hat from where he'd left it on her dresser, settled it on his head and picked up his stuff. "I'd best be on my way."

"I'll walk you to the door." She followed him out.

He managed to keep himself moving by blocking the image of that painting. At the door, he turned back to her. "If you ever need anything repaired, just let me know."

"Thank you, but I don't want to impose."

"It wouldn't be an imposition." Touching the brim of his hat, he let himself out the door. He didn't wish maintenance issues on anyone, but if she happened to have a few minor ones, that would give him an excuse to see her again.

He wouldn't get his hopes up, though. Like his mom had said, Olivia had lost her soulmate and even though his picture didn't sit on her bedside table, that didn't mean she was ready to move on.

2

Leaning next to a window that looked out on the front yard, Olivia watched Trevor drive away. She hadn't wanted him to leave. There, she'd admitted it. For the first time since Edward died, she'd looked at a man with a tiny bit of lust in her heart.

Okay, more than a tiny bit, and involving other body parts besides her heart. Her nerves jangled with a combination of excitement and uneasiness. What a surprise to discover she wasn't completely dead inside.

And why Trevor? He hadn't suddenly appeared on the scene. She'd known him casually for seven years.

This was her first interaction with him since he'd returned from Texas, though, and that trip seemed to have changed him in subtle ways. He was more focused, as if those six months had given him a sense of purpose.

It was there in his eyes, the color that was known around town as McGavin blue. It was there in the confidence he'd shown in tackling the repair.

Kendra had said he'd been handy with tools from an early age, but hiring on with Paladin Construction would logically have increased his skill level. He'd certainly been in control of that patch job.

She didn't have much experience with guys who could fix things. Her dad taught history and could recite major dates and events from memory, but he didn't know one end of a screwdriver from the other. Edward hadn't been handy, either.

Returning to her bedroom, she examined the wall and couldn't find the exact spot he'd repaired. He'd looked so good doing it, too. Capable hands, broad shoulders, back muscles flexing under his Western shirt, tight buns.

She hadn't studied a man at close range in a very long time. Because he'd been facing the wall, she'd been able to enjoy the view without giving anything away.

At least not intentionally. He might have read too much into her choice of artwork and paint color and who could blame him? Eros and *La Séduction* made it seem as if she had sex on the brain.

She most certainly did not. She'd merely been drawn to an unusual abstract and had wanted to highlight the dominant color with new paint.

Or was she kidding herself? She hoped to hell she wasn't. Life was much easier without those pesky yearnings. She'd had a generous supply of loving sex with Edward even if they'd only been married a few short years. She'd had more than some women got in a lifetime.

No other man had touched her in a sexual way. Letting Trevor do the things that Edward had done would be…uh-oh. She was getting hot. That was *not* something she wanted to deal with!

In minutes, she was out the front door and striding purposefully toward her destination. She always took a different route so she wouldn't create a telltale path through the wild grass.

The house backed up against the forest, but the acreage in front of it was covered with low brush and very few trees. The undulating terrain made sense to her now. It fit what lay underneath.

Anyone walking in this direction could miss the hole in the earth. She and Edward had passed it countless times in total ignorance. One summer afternoon he'd spotted it, though, and she considered it his discovery.

After spending the evening researching online, they'd driven into town the next day to buy ropes and hats. The metal stake they'd driven into the ground that day was still there, overgrown with wild grass as they'd intended it would be.

She glanced around before approaching the hole. It might be an unnecessary precaution because technically no one should be trespassing on her land, but she always checked.

No one was there. Good. On her way through the laundry room she'd picked up the coil of rope and miner's hat she kept on top of the dryer. Securing the rope to the stake, she put on her hat, turned on the light and dropped to her stomach on the dry grass.

After testing the rope with a firm tug, she started down. The opening was still a tight fit, but deeper down she and Edward had enlarged it and created footholds leading to the floor of the cave.

The entrance tunnel sloped gradually, allowing her to brace her feet against the side as she descended. Although she was plagued with a fear of heights, dropping slowing into the darkness didn't bother her at all.

Not being able to see much took away the fear for some reason. When her foot touched the limestone at the bottom, she let go of the rope and let it dangle against the damp earth.

She and Edward had been out of shape when they'd started this adventure. Eventually they'd built up their strength so they could make it up and down with only one stop in the middle. Thanks to kickboxing class, now she could do it without pausing.

One light didn't illuminate as well as two, but she knew her way around. She headed for the opening into the next chamber and crawled through.

Once there, she sat on a smooth limestone boulder. Larger chambers opened off this one, but she liked it here the best. She glanced around, checking the familiar formations for any sign of disturbance.

A drop of moisture glistened on the tip of a peach-colored stalactite. Holding her breath, she watched the drop fall to the stalagmite growing beneath it. The miracle never failed to inspire her.

She wasn't a geologist and Edward hadn't been, either. But they'd figured out immediately they'd stumbled on something special, something that needed protection. The steady dripping indicated a cave that was still alive, still growing. The flutter of wings meant a population of bats lived here. They'd found no evidence of humans.

Searching the internet, they'd bookmarked the website for Kartchner Caverns, a living cave in Arizona. The two hikers who'd discovered it had kept the secret for years until they'd finally negotiated with the state to secure protection for the delicate resource.

She and Edward had vowed to take the same care with their discovery. Then he'd gotten sick. For months, the cave had been the last thing on her mind, but eventually, after Edward died, she'd started coming back. This was where she felt closest to him. Where she talked to him.

"Hi, sweetie." She leaned back against a slab of cool stone behind her. "You know that hole I made in the drywall by accident?" She hugged her knees. "It's fixed, now."

The bats rustled and chirped in the next chamber and the cave continued its steady drip, drip, drip. The familiar sounds calmed her.

Still, her voice wasn't quite steady. "But here's the thing. The guy who fixed it was...Trevor McGavin." Speaking his name sent a tingle up her spine. "You remember him? He and Bryce are twins. Bryce is the guitar player we used to listen to at the Guzzling Grizzly."

She paused, not sure she was ready to say the next part out loud. Then she took a quick breath. "I'm...attracted to him. And I don't want to be." That second statement wasn't quite true.

Trevor had given her a jolt of welcome energy that coursed through her even now.

"Anyway, I'm feeling confused and out of sorts. But it doesn't change anything. I love you. And no matter what does or doesn't happen with Trevor, no one could ever replace you."

She breathed in the moist air. "I've also realized it's time to get moving on this project. This is such a special place. It means a lot to both of us. And it's up to me to figure out how to protect it. I'll proceed carefully and make sure I can trust anyone I talk to, but I have to get started."

She stood. "Okay, sweetie. Time to feed the horses. I'll be back soon. Take care." After crawling through the opening into the next room, she grasped the rope. The climb up was more work than going down and she was breathing hard by the time she reached the surface.

She poked her head up like a groundhog. The coast was clear, so she levered herself out of the hole and brushed dirt off her clothes. Then she coiled the rope and detached it from the metal stake. She'd just promised Edward that she'd move forward on the cave project. The trick was knowing where to start.

* * *

Trevor was lucky enough to walk into the Guzzling Grizzly during the Saturday afternoon lull—after the lunch crowd had cleared out and before the evening party folks had shown up. Even better, Bryce was the only person behind the bar.

Sliding onto a stool, Trevor looked around for the other bartender. "Where's Mike?"

"He's taking an online course and had some homework to finish. Want a draft?"

"Please." Trevor accepted the foam-topped mug with gratitude. "An online class, huh? What subject?"

"Small business management."

"No kidding? That says a lot about his dedication."

"Sure does. It was totally his idea, too. He's going to make one hell of a business partner."

"Have you closed the deal with Lou?"

"Should finalize it next week."

Trevor put down his beer and spread out his arms. "And all this will be yours."

"And Mike's. I'm giving him the apartment upstairs since I don't need it anymore. He's putting the rent money he'll save toward his share of the business."

"Nice deal for him."

Bryce laughed. "He thought so, too, although he insisted on getting internet installed up there."

"Just up there? You need it down here, too, bro. For customers."

"Mike's way ahead of you. We'll have free Wi-Fi by next week and a website. He's looking at those digital order pads, too, which would streamline things if we get as busy as he thinks we might. He's said from the beginning that this place has the potential to be a gold mine."

"That's awesome." Trevor lifted his mug. "Here's to Mike."

"Yeah, he's impressing me. Mandy's helping him design the website. She insisted on taking pictures of Nicole and me to jazz it up."

"Can't wait to see it. You're going to put us on the map."

"Hope so. Bringing more revenue to town would be a good thing for everyone."

"Absolutely."

"You had that repair job for Mrs. Shaw today, right?"

"Just finished it."

"How'd the house look?" He grabbed a rack of clean beer mugs and began polishing and stacking them in the pyramid style he favored.

"Same on the outside. Different inside. She likes bright colors and plants."

"She does? I'd never guess that from the way she dresses."

"I think that's her accounting outfit." He took a sip of his beer.

"Could be. I wonder if she has bright colors in her house to cheer herself up. Color affects your mood."

"Right." And his was still jacked up over all that pink. Her decision to redecorate could be a sign that she was recovering from her loss. Otherwise she might have chosen to leave the bedroom exactly the way it had been when Edward was alive.

He glanced at Bryce. "Do you think Mom and Dad were soulmates?"

"Probably. Why?"

"Thinking about Olivia's situation made me wonder about Mom's. She was young when

Dad died, too. And all these years later, she's never dated. Is that because Dad was her one true love?"

Bryce polished another mug and started the third level of the pyramid. "That might be part of it. She also told me that she hadn't wanted to take a chance on bringing some guy into our lives only to find out he was an asshole. Dating when you have kids can be tricky."

"But we're not kids anymore. In fact, she wouldn't have to worry about ending up with an asshole. If she did, we could kick his butt."

Bryce laughed. "You want to fix her up with somebody?"

"No, I just...why do you think she doesn't date?"

"Could be a lot of reasons." He picked up another mug. "She's been on her own for a long time. She might like it that way."

"Oh, she definitely likes being in charge. But the right guy would be okay with her being bossy."

That made Bryce grin. "Finding him might be tough, though. Eagles Nest is growing, but it's still a small town. Not a lot of eligible bachelors to choose from."

"You been keeping a tally?"

"Not exactly, but I suppose it's in the back of my mind. I meet a lot of people and so do you. Have you seen anybody who looked right for her?"

Trevor shook his head. "Can't say I have."

"The other roadblock could be us. Even though we're grown, we're a close family. She might wonder how that would change if she brought a stepdad into the mix."

"That's easy. If he makes her happy, we'd be happy for her. If he doesn't, out he goes. We'd see to it."

"Then ask her about it." Bryce gave him an amused glance. "See what she says. Then report back."

"I will, smartass." He sipped his beer and watched Bryce finish his pyramid. "Obviously having us was a major factor. Seems like if a widow has no kids and still doesn't date, it's gotta be the soulmate thing."

Bryce turned around and gazed at him. "I assume we're talking about the widow Shaw."

Trevor winced. "You make her sound like she has a stick up her ass. She takes kickboxing classes once a week in Bozeman."

"No shit." Bryce leaned against the counter. "And that fascinates you. Gonna test the soulmate thing and ask her out?"

"Don't know."

"Yeah, you do. I haven't seen that look in your eye for months."

"Maybe I caught the bug from you, lover boy." Trevor finished off his beer and stood. "I heard a rumor you and Nicole might sing a couple of duets tonight when the band takes a break."

"You heard right. Think you could come by?"

"I'll be here. But I'm on call tonight, so if I suddenly bolt, don't take it personally."

"You could invite the widow Shaw."

"I wouldn't ask her out when I'm on call. It's too soon, anyway. And stop calling her that."

"Just testing to see how much you like her."

"I like her. The operative question is whether she likes me."

"Don't let that soulmate business spook you, bro. You have one important advantage over her late husband."

"What's that?"

"You're alive."

Trevor chuckled. "Thanks. I'll be sure to work that angle."

Several hours later, showered, changed and with one of his mom's excellent meals in his belly, he walked back into the GG. Dinner had been a boisterous affair with Zane, Mandy, Cody and Faith gathered around the ranch's large dining table. Not the time to bring up the subject of his mom's dateless history.

When he'd announced that Bryce and Nicole were singing during the break, everyone decided to join him at the GG. He led the parade inside and helped Zane push two tables together and arrange the chairs. Drinks were ordered and delivered as the band finished its first set.

When the lead guitarist announced who would be filling in during the break, the place erupted. Trevor whistled and stomped as loud as anyone. Bryce handed Nicole up to the stage. Damn, those two looked great together.

Nicole wore a slinky black dress Mandy had designed for her and Bryce had his Johnny Cash look going on. Nicole had taken to wearing a black hat similar to Bryce's. Against all that black, her red curly hair stood out like a beacon.

Trevor leaned toward Cody. "I have five bucks that says they're gonna do *Jackson*."

"I'm not taking that bet." Cody thumbed back his hat. "It'll be *Jackson*."

Zane threw a five on the table. "*Islands in the Stream*."

"*It's Your Love*." Mandy dug a five out of her purse.

Faith shook her head. "I can't believe you're betting on this."

"Makes it more interesting." Trevor added his five to the pile and so did Cody.

Faith rolled her eyes. "It's already interesting, seeing Bryce up there when everybody thought he'd quit for good. Right, Kendra?"

"Right, Faith." But she tossed a five on the table. "*Islands in the Stream*."

When Bryce and Nicole launched into *Jackson*, Trevor high-fived Cody. Then he soaked up every bit of the amazing performance. Bryce had gone through hell with Charity, the ex-fiancée who'd bailed on their wedding day. He deserved the happiness he'd found with Nicole.

When they finished, the applause was deafening. Good thing he'd put his phone on vibrate, because otherwise he would have missed the text.

He shoved back his chair. "Gotta go." His gaze swept the table. "You should, too. Monitor the app I downloaded to everyone's phone. It's a wildfire."

His mom gasped. "Anywhere near the ranch?"

"No, but it sounds like it's too damned close to Olivia's place."

3

Olivia had spent the evening baking chocolate chip cookies, one of her favorite ways to relax. She'd also reviewed the website for Kartchner Caverns and taken notes on how the two men who'd discovered it had proceeded to get state support.

Then she'd climbed into bed with a book in hopes that would make her sleepy. No such luck. She wasn't getting drowsy and she couldn't concentrate on the story, either.

Trevor might as well have been in the room with her. His virility taunted her. When she closed her eyes, there he was, smiling at her, offering to take care of any future repairs. She was ready to break something just so he could fix it.

With a groan of frustration, she tossed the book aside. Her grandmother used to tell her *this too shall pass.* It was a lie. Her grief over Edward hadn't passed. It had dulled, but it wasn't gone. She missed him as much as ever.

Didn't she? Like a person flexing an injured limb, she stretched her grief muscle, expecting pain. Barely there. Huh.

Only one reason for that. Trevor McGavin had temporarily numbed her to the agony of losing Edward. She didn't want to be numb to it. Her pain was evidence that she continued to love him.

Maybe she shouldn't have redecorated the bedroom. Edward would have balked at all this pink. And what about the new mattress and bedframe? He wouldn't have chosen a fluffy pillow-top or a headboard stenciled with vines and flowers.

But she'd never liked the bed they'd chosen. The extra firm mattress was like sleeping on a board and the dark wood headboard with matching dressers and bedside tables weren't to her taste, either. Edward had loved dark wood and a firm mattress. His enthusiasm had charmed her into going along with his choice.

Getting rid of the bedroom furniture and buying something in honey oak had been hard. Replacing the mattress with something softer had been incredibly difficult, too. She'd made several visits to the cave during that time. But she slept better with a softer mattress and lighter colors around her. Or she had until tonight.

She switched off the lamp, snuggled under the covers and took deep, calming breaths. A cool breeze wafted through her partially open window and caressed her cheek. It could be Edward giving her a soft goodnight kiss.

Slowly she began to relax. Maybe she'd be able to sleep, after all...

Bang, bang, bang! Jerked from a dream about Trevor, she leaped out of bed and stood in the middle of the floor trembling.

Bang, bang, bang! "Mrs. Shaw!" A deep voice. Unfamiliar.

"What?" She tried to yell it but it turned into a squeak of fear. An intruder wouldn't bang on her door and call her Mrs. Shaw. She cleared her throat and tried again. "What?"

"Wildfire! You need to evacuate!"

The words buzzed around her, not penetrating, not making sense. Evacuate? She wasn't even dressed.

"Mrs. Shaw!" More pounding. "I'll break in if I have to!"

She smelled wood smoke. Wrenching open the closet door, she yanked a robe from a hanger and shoved her arms into it. She tied the sash on the way to the door.

"Mrs. Shaw!"

She unlocked the door, swung it open and stared at a man dressed in a yellow suit of some kind. A second man in yellow stood behind him.

"You have to get out now."

She vaguely recognized Javier Ortega, the ENFD chief, although she'd never seen him wearing all that protective gear. "I have...I have horses." Bonnie and Clyde.

"We know. McGavin's getting them out."

"Trevor McGavin?" Maybe it was all a crazy dream.

"Yes, ma'am. Bring me your truck keys and we'll hitch up your trailer."

"Right." This was happening. She raced to the hall closet, grabbed the keys from her purse and hurried back to the front door.

Ortega took the keys she thrust at him and tossed them to the man behind him. Then he glanced at her bare feet. "Put on shoes and close any open windows. Trevor will load your horses, but we need you to drive them out of here. Can you do that?"

She'd never pulled a trailer before. Edward had taken charge of that. But she couldn't let those horses down. "I'll be right back."

She ran to the bedroom and shut the window before shoving her feet into an old pair of canvas deck shoes and grabbing her glasses from the nightstand. Then she snatched her purse from the closet on the way to the front door. "Will my house burn?"

"I hope not, ma'am."

"Can I take a moment to gather a few things?"

"No. Sorry."

Photo albums, computer files, the pillow her grandmother had hand-stitched as a wedding present...

"Let's go. Lock your door."

"Right." She put on her glasses, flipped the lock on the knob and walked out on the porch. Taking the time to engage the deadbolt seemed stupid when the whole thing might burn down. And the cave? What would happen to it?

An enormous red fire truck was parked in her front yard. Two men dressed like the chief were unrolling a hose. The *whomp, whomp,*

whomp of rotary blades whirled overhead. She glanced up. "Helicopters?"

"Yes, ma'am." He hustled her toward her truck. "Dropping water."

Her robe came untied. Didn't matter. She saw the fire now, an orange glow through the trees, lighting the night sky. Another man in a yellow suit led Bonnie and Clyde toward the trailer. Trevor. "I sh-should help him."

"He's got it. Get in the truck, please."

She obeyed. Trevor knew horses. He could handle this. The clatter of hooves on the ramp told her he was loading them. All she had to do was start the truck and drive away once Bonnie and Clyde were in. A metal clang told her they were secure.

Trevor's shout confirmed it. "All clear! Take off, Olivia!"

Her hand shook as she dug through her purse for the keys. Why couldn't she find them?

The driver's door opened. "You okay?"

She glanced at someone who sounded like Trevor but the yellow suit made him look like he was from outer space. Those blue eyes belonged to Trevor, though. "I can't...f-find my k-keys." Her teeth chattered.

"They're in the ignition."

"Oh." She gulped. "Thanks." Hands shaking, she managed to turn the key. The engine started, but when she stepped on the gas, the truck didn't move. "What's wrong?"

"It's in Park."

"Oh."

"Do you need me to drive the truck?"

Yes. But he had important work to do. "N-no." She put her foot on the brake and adjusted the gearshift.

"Are you sure you're okay to drive?"

She focused on those blue eyes and dragged in a breath. "I can do it. Where should I go?"

"Mom's. She's expecting you."

"Stay safe."

"You, too."

"Head to Mom's. I'll see you there later." He closed the door and patted the side of it.

She gave him a nod, took her foot off the brake and gently bore down on the gas pedal. The drag from the trailer was considerable and she had to press harder. Okay, rolling now. Her heart hammered and her hands were slippery on the wheel.

Glancing in the rearview mirror, she watched the trailer as she made a gradual turn onto their dirt road. Thank heaven she'd had it graded recently.

She crawled toward the highway because she didn't know what would happen when she put on the brakes. How had Edward handled braking with a loaded trailer? She should have paid more attention, should have insisted on trying it herself.

Sweat trickled down her backbone and her stomach churned as she approached the highway. *Please let it be clear.* It was. She rolled right onto it without stopping.

People must have heard about the fire and were staying off the roads. She had it mostly to herself. The few vehicles she encountered either found a way to pass her or were headed in the opposite direction.

Nobody honked at her for driving under the speed limit. Other than the helicopters that flew overhead a couple of times, she made the trip in silence. She crept along, keeping the needle under twenty miles an hour.

The road through town was almost deserted, too. She caught one green light and rolled through a yellow. She took the dirt road to Wild Creek Ranch even slower. Coasting in at about five miles an hour, she barely had to touch the brakes to bring the truck to a stop in front of the main barn.

Slowly she unclenched her fingers from the steering wheel. Made it. She leaned her head back, not sure she had the strength or coordination to unlatch her seatbelt.

When had she fastened it? Trevor must have done it for her while she'd been freaking out.

The driver's side door opened. Faith stood there, looking concerned. "Cody's unloading your horses."

"Good. Thanks."

"Come on inside. Kendra's making up a bed for you."

"Oh, she doesn't need to do that." Olivia roused herself with an effort and managed to take off her seatbelt after a couple of tries. "I'll only be here a few hours."

"Well, yeah, probably." Faith sounded doubtful.

"No, really. They'll put that fire out in no time and I can go back." But not with the horses. Somebody else would have to trailer them home.

"Absolutely." Faith's enthusiasm sounded hollow. "But Kendra has the room and she likes to mother people."

"I know." Kendra had been more help than most when Edward died, possibly because she'd gone through a similar tragedy in her twenties. "And to be honest, I could use some mothering. Fire is scary."

"The scariest."

As she started to climb down from the truck, her leg gave way. If Faith hadn't grabbed her arm she would have fallen.

"Sorry. Guess I'm a little wobbly."

"You had a shock. Just take it slow."

Making her way with more care, she got both feet on the ground. "Oh, wait." The keys. And her purse. "I need to get my—"

"I'll get it. Lean against the truck. What do you need me to pull out?"

"Just the keys and my purse. That's all I have." She took Faith's advice, leaned against the side of the truck and waited.

"Here you go." Faith handed her the purse. "I put the keys in the front pocket."

"Thanks. I don't know why I should be so weak."

"Like I said, you had a shock and then you had to drive over here by yourself."

"I've never pulled a horse trailer before."

"Never?"

"Edward always did it. Since he died I haven't taken the horses anywhere."

"Hey, congratulations on accepting that challenge. That takes guts." Faith tucked an arm around her waist. "Come on. We can make some tea, or maybe you want something stronger."

"Tea sounds nice." She focused on walking, a task that seemed more difficult than it should be. "You've probably driven loaded horse trailers a lot."

"I have, but it's never a piece of cake. Hauling a live animal in a trailer takes some getting used to."

"I didn't know how to judge the braking part."

"So what did you do?"

"I was lucky. I went real slow and never had to use the brakes."

"Wow. I'm getting a picture of what the drive over must have been like. I'll bet you tensed every single muscle in your body."

"Probably."

"Maybe I should have put the horses in the barn and let Cody carry you into the house."

"I wouldn't have let him. Too embarrassing."

"Want to ride piggyback?"

Laughter poured out of her in a welcome rush. "Because that wouldn't be weird at all."

Faith grinned, revealing a small gap between her front teeth that made her look adorable. "I could take you as far as the porch. Nobody ever has to know."

"Thanks, but I'm feeling stronger, now."

"You look stronger. Your color's better."

"Good." She retied the sash on her robe. "It doesn't help that I had to face this wearing my nightgown and a bathrobe. Why is it that a crisis always hits right when you're at your most vulnerable?"

"Because it's a test."

"That's brilliant."

Faith shrugged. "Probably not. Maybe I read it on the back of a box of teabags. There. You've made it to the path. Clear sailing from now on."

"If my house burns down, I won't have anything to wear but this nightgown and bathrobe."

"Your house isn't going to burn."

"How do you know?"

"Trevor won't let that happen."

Olivia smiled. "Are McGavins that powerful?"

"Yes."

As she walked in the door and Kendra rushed to hug her, she was inclined to believe it.

4

Immersed in the battle against the fire, Trevor had no chance to find out whether Olivia had arrived safely. The uncertainty was a persistent ache in his gut. She'd been rattled and had driven away with a distinct lack of confidence. As if she'd never pulled a loaded horse trailer before.

He hadn't stopped to question that decision by Ortega. She owned the horses and a trailer. Logically she'd be able to use it to haul the animals out of harm's way.

Removing them from the scene had been critical. Despite the efforts of reinforcements from Bozeman and Billings, the fast-moving fire had gobbled the old barn with its dry timbers and loft full of hay. Trevor, Bryce and Jeremy had played in that hayloft.

As helicopters dumped buckets of water on the nearby forest, the ENFD crew turned its attention to saving the house. Trevor climbed to the roof with a backpack water bag and doused any sparks that landed on the shingles.

He lost track of how many times he climbed down to refill the bag and monitor hotspots. The crews on the ground managed to beat back the fire so it no longer threatened the structure, but the wind continued to blow sparks on the vulnerable roof. As a smoky dawn arrived, he started up the ladder again.

Ortega laid a restraining hand on his shoulder. "That's enough, McGavin. It's under control."

Backtracking to the ground, he gazed at the altered landscape. Only a smoldering pile of ashes remained where the barn had once stood. He didn't look forward to Olivia seeing that.

All vegetation had been cleared within twenty yards of the house, making the property appear abandoned. Anything that hadn't been chopped back had been mowed down by thick tires and heavy boots. But the house hadn't burned.

Huge swaths of pines and aspens behind the house were gone, which added to the starkness of the scene. Some tall pines remained, their trunks blackened and only a few tufts of green left at the top.

Ortega let out a sigh. "We were lucky. Next time you see Ryker, tell him thanks for me."

"Ryker?"

"He was flying in last night and spotted the fire. By hitting it early, we kept it relatively small."

"I'll make it a point to see him. And buy him a beer."

"You do that. Take him and April out for a nice meal. Charge it to the department." He glanced over as a fire truck lumbered into the front yard. "Fresh crew from Bozeman. Let's go home."

The ride back to the station seemed to take forever, but Trevor didn't want to call his mom until he could find a private corner. The minute they arrived he ducked into a storage area and pulled out his phone.

His mom answered on the first ring. "How are you?"

"I'm fine. Is Olivia okay?"

"She's okay, son."

"Thank God. When she drove out with that trailer she looked real shaky."

"Turns out she'd never done it before."

He closed his eyes. "Damn."

"But she made it. And she's finally asleep or I'd have you talk to her."

"No worries. I'll be home soon. She's gonna hate how the place looks, but we saved the house."

"Good."

"The barn's gone, though."

"Better that than the house."

"I know. It's just that it was a pretty little piece of property and now it looks like a war zone."

"It'll grow back. I'll help her plant new stuff."

"Good idea." His spirits lifted, as they usually did when he talked to his mom. Her resilience was her super power. "And guess who spotted the fire and called it in?"

"Ryker. He and April came over. Everyone was here. We kept track of things with that app you installed on my phone."

"Are they still there?"

"No. When the fresh crew came in from Bozeman, they all decided the show was over. That's when Olivia finally conked out."

"Where's she sleeping?"

"I gave her Cody's old room."

"Good choice. By the way, does she know her barn's gone?"

"I think she gathered that. She also figured out that her house was still standing. That's probably why she was finally able to sleep."

"You probably need to sleep, too."

"I will, right after I feed the animals. Zane, Cody, Faith and Mandy promised to meet me down at the barns in about ten minutes so we can get 'er done. We should be finished before you get here, so sweet dreams."

"I'll be extra quiet coming in. Love you, Mom."

"Love you, too, son."

He disconnected the call. The showers were running as the crew washed away the soot. He stripped down and did the same although he didn't bother shaving. Some of the guys were still on rotation and grabbed food or crashed in their bunks. Others had responded to the emergency call and were free to go home.

He had a bunk assigned but he wasn't required to sleep in it except for the two nights a week he'd agreed to stay in the firehouse. He toweled off, dressed in the clothes he'd been wearing when he'd left the GG, and drove away from the station bound for Wild Creek Ranch.

He hated that the fire had done so much damage to Olivia's place, but he was glad to have been there. Normally the ENFD didn't have volunteers. Back in August, he'd talked Ortega into taking him on.

They'd worked out a schedule that meshed with Trevor's construction job, which meant night shifts, only. Three nights a week he was on call and two nights a week he spent at the station house.

The schedule changed every week depending on where the chief had gaps. Gradually Trevor was learning all the jobs and the guys seemed to love having a rotating volunteer who eventually would be able to fill in for anybody.

Some of his friends didn't understand why he'd donate his time and risk his safety. His mom and his brothers got it, though. His passions were building things and enjoying the beauty of his native state. Fire threatened both, so he was learning how to fight it.

Money had never been a driving force in his life. But he'd made more in Texas than he was used to and he'd been inspired to open a savings account at the Eagles Nest National Bank. He hadn't been clear what he was saving for.

The intense hours he'd spent defending Olivia's house had sharpened his purpose. He wanted to build his own home. Cody and Faith had constructed a cute little A-frame on a forested section of ranch property, but he wanted more than that—his own land and a house of his design.

He'd probably build a barn, too. After growing up with horses, he'd like a couple. Pulling into the parking space beside the ranch house, he looked at it with new eyes.

His house would be log construction like this one, but he might go up another story. Stairs were cool. And a porch. Had to have a porch. And a stone fireplace. Maybe a back deck with a hot tub.

He walked up the path to the house and climbed the steps carefully, mindful of the third one that squeaked. He'd fix that now that the second barn was done. If his mom would make a list of the nagging little maintenance chores she needed, he'd work his way through them.

But regardless of whether he was framing a house for Paladin Construction or keeping the ranch buildings in good repair, he was still working on a structure that didn't belong to him. He'd be happy to continue doing those things if he also had something of his own, something he could mold into any shape he wanted.

Until this moment, he hadn't acknowledged how strong that craving was. Opening the front door, he walked into the living room and turned around to close the door. When he swung back, he froze in place. Olivia stood in the hallway.

Her sudden appearance startled him. He'd expected her to be asleep, but she must have been listening for him to come home. He had info she wanted.

Her jeans and sweater had prompted an adjustment in his thinking, but this outfit required a total overhaul of his assumptions about Olivia

Shaw. Her satin robe and nightgown matched the erotic pink of her bedroom walls. If that was accidental, he'd eat his hat.

She wore her glasses, but that was all that was left of her accountant persona. Her dark hair tumbled around her shoulders in glorious abundance. If she took off her robe and nightgown, she could drape her hair over her breasts.

Heaven help him, he ached for her to do that. He wanted her in his arms, her silky hair sliding over his naked body. He shivered. Maybe exhaustion was making him hallucinate, because something in her eyes told him that he wasn't the only one with that idea.

She drew in a breath. "You saved my house."

"Not just me. Plenty of firefighters worked to save it." He took a few steps toward her.

"But you were the one who cared the most." She closed the gap a little more.

"Well, yeah. You're a family friend." Boy, didn't that sound dumb. He drifted closer.

She smiled. "You mean I'm the nice person who brings homemade cookies when I come to visit? The one who remembers everyone's birthday with an appropriate card?"

He laughed before he remembered he was supposed to be quiet. "*No.* I didn't mean that at all. You're…" He cleared his throat. "You're nothing like I thought you were. Let's leave it at that."

Her voice was soft and her gaze even softer. "Okay."

He was within touching distance. In his world, standing this close to a woman in sexy nightwear meant they were about to make love. Not today.

He couldn't even assume she was trying to be provocative. She'd arrived in this outfit and it was opaque enough to be perfectly decent. Except chances were good she wore nothing underneath.

He swallowed. Time to get the main points of this conversation out of the way so he could go to his room and she could return to Cody's. "I'm sorry about your barn. It was right in the path and we had to let it go."

"I heard."

"Mom can keep your horses until you build a new one."

"She already told me that and I'm very grateful. I'm sure Bonnie and Clyde will have a blast hanging out with all these horses."

"Bonnie and Clyde? Aren't they both geldings?"

"Yes, but Edward and I had decided on those names when we still lived in Chicago. Once we got out here we learned that two geldings made more sense for beginners than a gelding and a mare. But we kept the names, anyway."

"I see." It helped cool his jets to hear her talk about Edward with affection. "You were very brave to take the horses out when you'd never pulled a trailer."

"My horses, my job." She nudged her glasses more firmly into place and lifted her chin. "The rest of you had work to do. Taking someone away from that because I couldn't handle my responsibility would have been wrong."

She had courage. Too bad he was a sucker for gutsy women. "I realized you were scared, though. I even suspected you were hauling horses for the first time, but I—"

"You had to let me do it." She took a deep breath. "And I did. But before I pull another loaded horse trailer, I intend to get some instruction."

"I'll be glad to teach you."

"That would be great."

Evidently he was still looking for ways to spend time with her, whether that was wise or not. "You probably know more than you think you do, since you made it over here."

"I know nothing. I drove the entire way without using my brakes."

"Whoa. Not at all?"

She shook her head and her dark hair rippled. "I went real slow and there was hardly any traffic."

"I guess there wouldn't be much. Most people try to stay off the road when there's a wildfire anywhere near town."

"How soon will I be able to go back?"

"I'm not sure. I can find out for you in a few hours, but my guess is they'll need to monitor the area for hotspots. They won't want you in there until it's safe."

"Today?"

"Maybe. I'm thinking not, though."

She deflated a little. "I was hoping."

"Listen, when you do go back." He hesitated. "Your house is perfectly fine, but the area around it took a hit."

Her gaze sharpened. "What about the acreage between the main road and the house?"

"The grassland? I don't think it was affected much."

"Good."

"But we had to clear off anything near the house that would burn."

"My flowers?"

"Had to go."

"My vegetable garden?"

"Did you have one?"

"Yes, in back. I'd harvested most of it but I still had…" Her voice trailed off. "I'm guessing it's gone, too."

"Sorry."

Her lower lip trembled.

"I'll help you plant a new one next spring."

She nodded. "It's just that Edward and I…" With a quick gulp, she turned away. "I'll…I'll see you later, okay?" She walked quickly down the hall and into Cody's room. The door closed with a soft click.

Sure as the world, she'd planted that garden with Edward. If there was any doubt whether she was still grieving, her reaction to losing the garden confirmed it. He scrubbed a hand over his face. She still loved her late husband. That didn't leave much room for another man.

5

Edward had loved that garden. Olivia shoved her face into the pillow so no one would hear her cry. Losing the garden hurt. It hurt more than losing the barn.

After she'd sobbed out the worst of her sadness and anger, she flopped to her back while tears dribbled across her cheeks and into her ears. After all Edward's struggles, the little plot was gone. How unfair.

In the beginning, he'd naively tried to grow veggies the way his grandmother had in Southern Illinois. He used to rhapsodize about picking huge tomatoes and squash from her garden when he was a kid.

They'd bought acreage here so he could recreate it. Except he hadn't had a gift for horticulture. Lack of talent combined with critter invasions and a short growing season produced poor yields. But he'd been persistent and by the third year he'd almost figured it out.

After he died, she'd kept the garden going and this summer had been the best yet. She'd shared some of the harvest with her clients, including Kendra. Sure, she could replant in the spring. Trevor had been kind to offer his help.

But if the firefighters had torn it out to save the house, then she'd have to start over. It wouldn't be Edward's garden anymore. Why bother?

She'd focus on the good news. The grassland hadn't been burned, which meant the cave and the bats might not have been affected. That was more important than Edward's garden. He would have said so, for sure.

The tears finally stopped. She'd never been a fan of crying. It made her throat hurt, her eyes swell and her nose run.

She grabbed a box of tissues from the bedside table and blew her nose. Better. She was physically and emotionally wiped out, but calmer. Nothing could be done now. Taking off her robe, she laid it across the end of the bed, crawled under the covers and went to sleep.

She woke to the sound of chickens clucking. Climbing out of bed, she put on her glasses and went to the partially open window. Kendra was out back feeding her flock.

She clearly loved those plump, fluffy birds. She talked to them as if they were close friends as she scattered feed in a slow circle around her.

The henhouse was gorgeous, too. Kendra had mentioned that Trevor had built it for her and like a proud mama she'd bragged about his carpentry skills. For good reason, too. The henhouse looked like a mini Victorian complete with a blue exterior and white gingerbread trim. It even had a front porch on either side of the ramp leading into it.

Watching the chicken-feeding ritual soothed Olivia's frayed nerves and she stayed where she was until Kendra collected the eggs and left the pen. Then she pushed up the window and called to her.

Kendra turned in her direction. "Did I wake you with the chickens?"

"You did, but I need to get up." She glanced at the sky. "It's late, huh?"

"Past five."

"What's the story about going back to my house? Do you know?"

"Trevor said you won't be able to tonight. The firefighters are still checking the surrounding area for hotspots. You're stuck here until tomorrow, at least."

"Oh." She'd expected it but that didn't make hearing it any easier.

"Since you'll be staying, I'll bet you could use a few things to make you feel more human, right?"

"That's putting it mildly."

"Let me bring in the eggs and then I'll gather up some clothes and toiletries for you. I think we wear roughly the same size. How about jeans and a long-sleeved t-shirt?"

"That would be great."

"Underwear will be trickier but I have a stretchy sports bra that should work and my panties should fit you."

"Thanks. I'm sure you never expected to be loaning your underwear to your accountant."

She smiled. "I'm not loaning it to my accountant. I'm loaning it to my friend."

"Aw." Her throat tightened.

"I have a nightgown you can borrow, too. I'll bet you're sick of wearing that one, pretty as it is."

"I used to like it, but now it might have to go."

Kendra laughed. "I understand. See you in a few minutes."

Putting on her robe, Olivia quickly made up the bed and opened her door. *Beef stew.* The aroma hit her full force and her stomach growled. Kendra had fed everyone snacks in the wee hours of the morning, but that food was a distant memory. Once Kendra brought her a change of clothes, she'd take the fastest shower in history if a bowl of stew awaited her at the end of it.

Leaning in the doorway, she peered down the empty hallway. All the bedrooms were in this section of the house. The master was at the far end with an attached bath. Three smaller bedrooms shared the hall bath.

During last night's ordeal, Trevor's brothers had regaled her with stories of epic battles over possession of that bathroom. The bedrooms had been another source of combat. In the beginning, Ryker and Zane each had a room. When Bryce and Trevor had arrived, they'd shared a room because they were twins, after all. Then Cody had come along.

Ryker and Zane had been crammed together and baby Cody had been given his own room. Nobody had thought that was fair except

Cody, the spoiled one. The teasing and laughter had helped carry Olivia through the long hours. Because she was an only child, she envied them a little, too.

Presently, that hall bathroom was occupied. Then the door opened and Trevor came out shirtless and clean-shaven. He blinked. "You're awake."

Oh, yes, she was. After getting a good look at his muscled chest lightly furred with dark hair, she was *so* awake. She was amazed that her glasses hadn't fogged. "I...um...your mother was feeding the chickens."

"It's their dinnertime."

She took a quick breath. "Right. She's also getting me some clothes to change into after I take a shower." Why did she feel the need to blurt that out?

"Good idea."

"Am I that stinky?"

"No! I meant the clothes are a good idea. Not that there's anything wrong with what you have on."

"I'm not in the habit of wearing a nightgown and bathrobe all the time." But she wouldn't mind if he'd ditch his shirt more often. Dear God, he was beautiful.

"At least they look nice." Then he turned red. "I mean, you could have been stuck with an ugly granny gown and that would have been worse." He cleared his throat. "You know what? I'm going to drop this conversational thread before I get any more tangled up in it."

"Okay." Gorgeous and flustered. What a dynamite combo.

"Did Mom mention that your property is still off-limits at least until tomorrow?"

"She told me." The scent of his shaving cream created a tingling sensation in her belly. She longed to stroke his freshly shaven cheek.

"I'm sure you're eager to get back."

"Yes and no." What woman in her right mind would be eager to leave when confronted with a bare-chested Trevor McGavin?

"I probably scared you a little with my description of the place."

"Some."

"I figured I should tell you, though."

"Oh, absolutely! I'm glad you warned me. I've never seen the aftermath of a fire except on the news." And she'd never seen a half-naked, muscular guy up close except in the movies. Edward had been on the lean side. She was mesmerized just watching Trevor breathe.

"The chief suggested I take you over there instead of just letting you go by yourself. But that's totally up to you."

"Don't you have to work tomorrow?"

"Normally, but Greg decided to give us Columbus Day off. What about you? Do you have client appointments?"

"I have one, but I should be able to move it to Tuesday. If you're available tomorrow, I'd appreciate having you along."

"Good." He motioned toward the bathroom. "It's all yours."

"Thanks, I—"

"Are you two negotiating bathroom privileges?" Kendra arrived with a bundle of clothes and a small canvas bag. She pretended to glare at them. "Because I won't tolerate any bickering."

Trevor let out a sigh. "Mom."

"Couldn't resist teasing you, especially after all the reminiscing last night about the bathroom wars."

"Nice." He rolled his eyes.

"It helped pass the time," Olivia said. "I especially loved the story of you installing a new doorknob and keeping the only key."

"It would have worked if Ryker hadn't passed his driver's test that day. My plan took weeks to set up, but he just drove into town, got a new doorknob and kept the key. He stole my strategy."

Olivia smiled. "He admitted it."

"He did?"

"He said you were one step ahead of him. He acted proud of the fact."

"Huh." Trevor seemed pleased by that.

"It was fun hearing those old stories." Kendra gazed at her son. "I love having adult children, but sometimes I miss those days. You boys were always up to something."

"And now we're boring?"

"No, just...mature."

"Which is code for boring. Guess it's time to break out the whoopee cushion and the plastic spiders."

"Please don't." Kendra patted his arm. "It was just an idle comment." She handed Olivia the clothes and bag of toiletries. "If anything doesn't fit, let me know. Mandy might have something better."

"I'm sure this will be fine. Thank you so much."

"Are you hungry?"

"Starving."

"Good. Everyone will be here around six. But if you can't wait that long, I'll—"

"I can wait that long. Who's coming?"

Kendra ticked them off on her fingers. "Ryker and April. Zane, Mandy and her mom, Jo. Cody and Faith. Nicole's playing tonight so she and Bryce can't make it, but otherwise it's the whole fam-damn-ly."

Olivia hugged the bundle of clothing to her chest. "If they're coming at six, I'd better grab a shower and make myself presentable."

"You're always presentable." Evidently that just popped out, because immediately Trevor got red and cast a quick glance at his mom. "She is, right? Every time she comes over she looks so professional."

"She certainly does." Kendra's eyes sparkled and she pressed her lips together.

"Thanks, but I don't feel particularly professional in this getup, so if you'll excuse me, I'm going to hit the showers." She started toward the bathroom.

Kendra and Trevor stepped aside, but the hall wasn't very wide. Trevor's masculine scent teased her as she passed by.

His breath hitched, as if he was equally aware of her. "Do you need me to show you how the shower works?"

"I can probably figure it out." She ducked into the bathroom, closed the door and leaned against it, heart thumping. Wowza.

She had no experience with wild sexual urges. Edward had been a friend for a long time before he became her lover. The transition had been gradual, almost inevitable. No uncertainty or awkwardness. No rush. Definitely no wildness.

Even her most passionate moments with Edward hadn't made her breathless and dizzy. She was both of those things as she pressed her back against the door and closed her eyes. The image of Trevor shirtless wouldn't go away.

She'd never separated love and sex before, never had to. She'd loved the only man she'd ever had sex with. Honesty forced her to admit that she wanted to have sex with Trevor even though she didn't love him.

She liked him. She liked him quite a bit. He was kind, thoughtful and brave enough to face a raging fire. He'd helped save her horses and her house. And he'd inspired a massive case of lust.

Could she have sex without love? The idea didn't sit right with her, so probably not. She'd have to resist temptation, even though it came packaged in the form of Trevor McGavin.

And speaking of packages....

Stop it! With a sigh, she stripped down and turned on the shower.

6

Trevor was always grateful for his family, but never more than tonight. He was dangerously close to obsessing over Olivia and the rowdy gathering provided exactly the distraction he needed.

His mom had made stew, but everyone else arrived with food, and that helped, too. If he couldn't satisfy one hunger, he'd satisfy another. The dinner table was loaded with choices and he intended to sample them all. He'd stuff himself until he was too full to care about sex.

Ryker and April brought a large dish of meatless lasagna that smelled delicious. Ryker, the guy who used to eat some form of beef nearly every night, had become quite a veggie lover. He wasn't quite ready to label himself a vegetarian. Not yet, anyway.

Zane and Mandy contributed barbequed ribs and slaw, one of Trevor's favorite combos. Cody and Faith had made fried chicken and a pot of beans. Faith fried the chicken extra crispy the way Trevor liked it. Aunt Jo had baked the biggest chocolate cake he'd ever seen.

Olivia, dressed in a pair of his mom's jeans and a purple shirt, took the chair Trevor held for her. He might have to shelve any plans to pursue her, but he could sit next to her at dinner while he ate his way to oblivion.

She stared at the feast piled on the oversized dining table. "Wow. Do you always eat this way?"

"Not always." Zane grinned at her from across the table. "Sometimes there's more."

Mandy gave him an elbow in the ribs. "Don't tease her."

"I'm not teasing. Sometimes there *is* more. Back me up, guys."

"He's right," Trevor said. "We're missing Bryce and Nicole. If they'd come, they would have brought food, too."

"Okay," Mandy said, "but still, this much food on the spur of the moment is unusual. I think we're all grateful the fire wasn't worse and nobody was hurt." She gestured toward the loaded table. "This is how we show it."

His mom tapped on her wine glass. "And I want to start things off by toasting my firefighting son. Here's to Trevor."

His face warmed as everyone lifted a bottle or a glass in his direction. "Thank you, but I was only—"

"Being a hero." Beside him, Olivia raised her wine glass. "To Trevor McGavin, who saved my house and my horses."

Everyone cheered and his brothers even stomped their boots under the table. It was embarrassing as hell, but nice, too. When the commotion died down, he raised his beer. "I have a toast. To Ryker, who spotted that fire from the air when it was still small. The chief told me to give you his thanks."

Another cheer went up and this time it was Ryker's turn to be embarrassed. "I was lucky," he said, his voice gruff. "Any of you would have done the same."

"Sure we would," Cody said. "Assuming we had a pilot's license, a plane and an eagle eye like you. Own your talents, big brother."

"Thanks, Cody." But the extra praise only made Ryker look more uncomfortable. "Hey, could we eat, now?"

"We sure can." His mom had the stewpot on a trivet in front of her, along with a stack of bowls. "Who wants some of this?"

"Me, please!" Olivia spoke up so quickly that Trevor chuckled.

"Hungry?" He gave her an amused glance.

She met his gaze. "You have no idea." Heat flared in her brown eyes.

For one electric moment, the world stopped. Then she looked away. The air left his lungs. Had he imagined that? Or did she want him as much as he wanted her?

The question plagued him throughout the evening. The jokes and laughter flew as always and he participated as best he could. But he kept coming back to that searing glance of hers. What did it mean?

He was in the kitchen fetching more beer for the table when Zane came in. Trevor handed him a couple of bottles. "Just in time to help me carry."

"I'm here to serve." Then he lowered his voice. "What's up?"

No point in brushing him off. His brother knew him too well. He glanced toward the dining room. The jokes and laughter should give him enough cover. "I'm...interested in Olivia."

"Tell me something I don't already know."

"But I can't figure her out."

Zane smiled. "That's never happened to me. When it comes to women, I have all the answers."

"Sure you do." Trevor took out three more beers and set them on the counter while he went into the pantry for another six-pack.

"But you need to give me more to go on if you want my excellent advice."

Trevor put the six-pack on the counter and faced him, keeping his voice low. "This morning she broke down because our crews destroyed the garden her husband planted. I took that to mean she still loves him and I'm SOL. Then tonight she gave me a look that would scorch the label off a beer bottle."

"That's easy. She still loves her late husband but she desperately wants to do you."

"And how am I supposed to respond to *that*?"

"Depends on what you want."

Trevor gazed at him. "That's the big question, isn't it?"

"Yep. Short-term gain or long-term reward."

"I'll have to think about it."

"Figured you did." Zane took the six-pack and opened the refrigerator. "Time to chill these puppies and get back to the party." He shoved the carton in the nearest empty space and closed the door.

"Hang on a minute. When Mandy came back to town, which were you after?"

"Short-term gain. She had her fashion design career in New York so I didn't think I had a chance for anything more. But..."

"But?"

"Deep down I had that long-term reward in mind. I just couldn't admit it."

"That's a bullshit answer."

"Not really. Sometimes you have to go for the short-term gain and see what happens."

"You are so full of it."

"She looks cute in Mom's clothes. She's not as stuffy as I thought."

"You should have seen her in a nightgown."

"Hot?"

"Oh, yeah."

Zane nodded. "Your face has short-term gain written all over it right now."

"Where's the beer, losers?" Ryker bellowed in his drill sergeant voice.

"Sir!" Zane winked at Trevor. "Coming immediately, sir!"

When Trevor walked in behind Zane, Olivia was laughing about something. Then he saw Cody balancing a spoon on his nose. Trevor had never seen her laugh like that, red-faced and gasping for breath. She had to take off her glasses and wipe her eyes.

He liked seeing her have fun, considering the trauma of losing her barn and nearly losing her house. What he wanted might not be all that important when stacked up against what Olivia needed. He wouldn't presume to make that decision, but if he paid attention, she might tell him.

Everyone stayed late, lingering over coffee and Aunt Jo's spectacular cake. Ryker built a fire to take away the slight chill and everyone gathered in the living room to enjoy it. Trevor absolutely would build a wood-burning fireplace in his home. People were drawn to it in an elemental way.

Midnight approached, and the leave-taking began. Trevor watched with a full heart, glad to be here. He belonged in Eagles Nest, where he could share a family dinner with the people he loved, where he knew the roads by heart and a good percentage of the townspeople.

He liked the certainty that he'd get a fair deal at George's Garage and a hearty meal at the Eagles Nest Diner. Pills and Pop had a soda fountain. Not many places did anymore.

Olivia had chosen to live here. She could have left after Edward died, but she hadn't. Instead she'd stuck it out, maintained the accounting business they'd started, and planted veggies and flowers.

He was determined that she'd plant again next spring, but first he had to get her over the shock of that first glimpse. He'd be there for that, thanks to the chief's suggestion and a holiday weekend.

If humanly possible, he'd be there every damn time she needed him. She'd been put through the wringer and had survived. No surprise that he was drawn to her after being raised by a woman who'd made it through similar circumstances.

After everyone had left, Trevor made sure the kitchen was shipshape before he walked into the living room. His mom and Olivia were deep in conversation, so he said goodnight and left them to their discussion. Then he quickly finished up in the bathroom so Olivia could have it to herself.

Their rooms were next to each other, but early this morning, when he'd been exhausted from fighting the fire, he hadn't cared. Tonight he was more rested. Tonight he cared.

Stripping off his shirt, he tossed it in the laundry hamper. He'd taken off his belt and started to unbutton his jeans when a soft knock at his door sent his pulse into overdrive.

His mom wouldn't knock softly. She'd rap on his door with the authority automatically granted to a mother, especially one as bossy as his. That left only one other possibility.

Olivia stood outside his door.

He took a quick breath. "I'm finished in there. You can have it."

"Thanks, but I...I wanted to talk with you." She glanced at his bare chest and her cheeks turned pink. "If it's okay."

"Sure. Want to come in?" Bad idea, but it seemed like the polite thing to say.

"Um, all right." She moved into the room with tentative steps and looked around. "You have bunk beds in here."

"There are bunks in the other room, too. Cody's the only one who got a double bed."

"Because he was spoiled rotten." She smiled.

"Exactly."

"I had a bunk bed." She wandered over to it. "Only mine was white. The idea was to invite my friends for sleepovers."

"Did you?" He'd had trouble concentrating when they'd been alone in her pink-toned bedroom with the erotic painting over the bed. It was ten times worse here when he was already half undressed. Two steps and he'd be right beside her.

"Sure, I invited people, and we had fun, but I was always on edge, trying to figure out the dynamic. Edward was an only child, too. When we moved in together, we both admitted it was the first time we hadn't felt alone."

He didn't want to hear that, but he needed to. "You must have had a close bond."

"Very close. I miss him every day."

"I'm sure."

"But that isn't what I wanted to talk to you about. Well, it is, in a way." She pulled a section of her hair forward and combed her fingers through it in what was clearly a nervous gesture. Once again she stared at his naked chest and blushed.

"Hold on a minute." Digging his shirt out of the hamper, he put it on and fastened the snaps.

He left the shirttails hanging out. No need to be anal about it. "Is that better?"

"Yes. Thank you."

"You're welcome." Her fascination with his pecs was flattering. If she suddenly stripped to the waist he'd have trouble carrying on a conversation, too.

Great. Now he had that image in his head. Not helpful.

She took a deep breath and met his gaze. "I decided honesty is the best policy, so here goes. I'm attracted to you."

That was the good news. He figured the bad news was coming next. Might as well meet it head on. "But you wish you weren't."

"That's right." Her breathing was becoming uneven. "Although it's exciting to feel this way."

"Yes, it is." She was giving him that look again, the same one from the dining table. Damn, she sure did get to him.

"But it's...it's only sex." She gulped. "I'll never love anyone but Edward."

"Understood."

"So having sex when I still love Edward isn't fair to you." She spoke the words quickly as if desperate to get them out.

"Let me be the judge of that." If short-term gain was all he could have, he'd take it. His body heated at the prospect.

She stared at him. "You'd be fine having sex with me when you know I'm still in love with Edward?"

"At the risk of having you think less of me, yes, I would."

She combed her fingers through her hair and looked away. "Well, I wouldn't be okay with it." Her tone softened. "I've never had sex without love."

Wow. He blew out a breath to release some of the tension. "Are you saying that Edward was your only—"

"Neither of us had been with anyone."

"I see." And he was so screwed.

When she looked at him again her gaze was pleading. "I know I've been giving off mixed signals and I apologize for that. I've never dealt with lust before."

Too bad it was such a serious discussion because that was funny. He'd insult her if he laughed, though, so he dialed it back. "Is there anything I can do?"

"That's just it. You can't help being so sexy."

He rubbed a hand over his mouth to cover a grin. Being kicked to the curb had never felt so good.

"This is my problem, not yours. I'll handle it, but I thought I should explain what was going on with me."

He cleared his throat. "Thanks."

"I'll see you in the morning." She started for the door.

"Does this mean you'd rather have someone else take you over to your place when you're cleared to go back? I'm sure someone else would be happy to do it if you think—"

"I'd rather have you." She glanced at him. "You were there so you're prepared. Anyone else would be seeing it for the first time, like me."

"Good point."

"I promise to behave myself."

He swallowed a laugh. "Don't do it on my account."

"See there?" She gestured toward him. "You're sexy without even trying." Groaning in obvious frustration, she hurried out the door and closed it behind her.

He stood very still and watched the door. If she was as worked up as he was, she'd charge back through it and throw herself into his arms.

But she didn't. Clearly that wasn't her personality. For the time being, she appeared to be serious about controlling her lust. Who did that these days when they had a willing partner? An exceedingly willing partner! Olivia Shaw, that's who.

7

Olivia got the call first thing the next morning. She could return home. She wanted to go, but leaving the comfort of the ranch wouldn't be easy. It had been a refuge.

Originally Trevor had planned to drive her there but that made no logistical sense. He'd only have to bring her back to the ranch so she could fetch her truck. Instead she asked him to follow her over so she wouldn't face the devastation alone.

Once she was settled in, he could head back to the ranch. Despite her embarrassing confession the night before, she still wanted him to come with her. His solid presence was the best insurance against freaking out.

After breakfast, she gave Kendra a hug and walked out to her truck. Trevor had borrowed her keys so he could park her trailer out of the way beside the new barn before he unhitched it. Then he drove her truck up to the front of the house and climbed out, leaving the driver's door open.

She walked around the front bumper. "Thank you so much. This is like valet parking."

"Yes, ma'am." He smiled and touched the brim of his hat. "Oh, wait. You don't like me to call you ma'am."

Except this time she'd been charmed by his use of it. "Evidently that depends on your delivery."

"Oh, does it, now? Care to explain that?"

Now she'd done it. She glanced up at him and heat swirled in her belly. Even shaded by his hat, his eyes cast a powerful spell. "I guess it's the difference between being formal and familiar."

"So the other day it sounded too formal?"

"In a way. It...I don't know...I guess it put distance between us."

His gaze warmed. "Lord knows I don't want that."

The distance between them was shrinking faster than a cotton shirt in boiling water. "Could you please stop flirting?" She swung up behind the wheel and laid her purse and a small canvas bag for her nightwear on the passenger seat.

"Probably not after what you said last night."

She turned to him. "I made it worse?"

"'fraid so. Want me to round up Zane to follow you over there? He's a married man. I guarantee he won't flirt."

"No, I want you to go with me."

"All righty, then." Digging his keys from his pocket, he tossed them in the air and caught them again. "Let's do this."

It was a purely male gesture. Evidently she was thrilled by any sexy move he made.

"Go ahead and pull out if you want. I'll be right behind you." He flashed her a smile and jogged over to the parking area beside the house to get his truck.

She watched him in the rearview mirror because, damn it, he looked good from the back, too. What was wrong with her? She'd never been one to ogle guys, but she couldn't stop doing it with Trevor.

When he got into his truck, she quickly buckled up and started the engine. One good thing about this hormonal reaction—it minimized her concern over her fire-damaged property.

Could that be Trevor's plan? Instead of flirting to be contrary, maybe he was hoping to distract her from worrying about what she was about to see. If so, it worked. All the way to her house, she was focused on the cowboy following her instead of the fire scene awaiting her.

Once she turned onto her road, though, she was jerked back to reality. The grading she'd recently paid for had been destroyed by the coming and going of heavy fire trucks. She bounced over deep ruts and slowed to a crawl.

But the grassland on either side of the road was untouched by fire, just as Trevor had said. What a relief.

She'd never researched how a fire could affect caverns located directly beneath it. Maybe they'd be protected, but she wouldn't bet on it. Ash would filter down. And if the cave had bats, as hers did, they might get confused and fly into the fire, or get trapped in the caves with the smoke.

However, judging from the evidence, the caves under her property were okay. She wouldn't have to deal with potential damage to the beautiful caverns or the resident bats.

But she did have to face...dear God. She rolled into her front yard, or what was left of it. She'd prepared herself for the barn to be gone, but not for the huge gaps in the forest where trees used to be. Trevor had hinted at it, but she'd had no idea...

Quiet. Why was everything so still? Oh. Normally the morning was filled with the chirp and twitter of hundreds of birds.

The smoke had cleared and blue sky was everywhere. Way too much sky and not enough green. Her throat tightened.

The trees had been huge. Those gaps wouldn't be filled for twenty years, maybe thirty. A few tall sentinels remained, their blackened trunks bearing witness to the violence they'd suffered.

Leaving her stuff on the seat, she climbed down from her truck. She couldn't even blame someone's carelessness. Although she'd never heard of a dry thunderstorm, the chief had said that was the only explanation. One must have come through several nights ago. A single lightning bolt had found a dead tree.

He'd talked to her about fire cycles and the necessity for them to keep the forest healthy. It had sounded reasonable and logical. But this raw carnage threatened her sense of place, her sense of self. This was no longer the same land where she and Edward had settled six years ago. That had been destroyed.

Trevor's strong arm circled her shoulders, but he didn't speak. She was grateful. When Edward had died, a few well-meaning souls had tried to comfort her with variations of *it was meant to be.*

If some cruel entity had taken Edward as part of a grand plan, that only made her more furious. If her little piece of heaven, her last connection with Edward, had been decimated to satisfy the greater good, then to hell with the greater good. She much preferred the slogan *shit happens.*

"Want to go in the house?"

"Not yet." Her voice was thick with tears. Her face was wet, too, but so what? "I don't care about the house, the barn, the garden or the yard. I care about the *forest.*"

His fingers tightened on her shoulder. "Me, too."

She took off her glasses and swiped at her eyes.

"Use this." He put a soft cotton bandana in her hand.

"Thank you." She dried her eyes and mopped her face. "If I stop wearing my glasses, everything will be blurry. That sounds like a great idea."

"Go ahead. I'll be your guide dog and make sure you don't bump into things."

She took a ragged breath. "Thanks, but it's time to pull on my big-girl panties."

"I've always wondered how they're different from little-girl panties." His tone was light, as if he hoped this silly topic would be a distraction.

It certainly could be. She'd play along. "Little-girl panties are decorated with cutsie stuff. Some have kittens and puppies. Some have the days of the week embroidered on them. Those were a major stressor for me. I had to wear the right ones on the right day."

"I'm not surprised."

"Yeah, you have me pegged."

"I doubt it."

"Yes, you do. I'm the shy one who joined the math club. The brainy one the cool boys didn't ask out. I had exactly one boyfriend and I married him."

Trevor grew quiet after that.

"I'm sorry. I shouldn't keep bringing him up."

"Yes, you should. It reminds me where I stand."

"I don't get it."

"Get what?"

"Why would a sexy cowboy like you be the least bit interested in me?"

He laughed. "You seriously underestimate yourself. Ready to go in the house?"

"I guess." She surveyed the muddy expanse between where she stood and the screened-in porch.

"I'll carry you."

"No, I—whoa!" She was in his arms before she could blink and on her way to the porch. "This is ridiculous." *And wonderful.* He was so warm. So close. Her heart was going a mile a minute.

"It's not ridiculous. This way only one of us ends up walking through mud."

"Then I'll clean your boots for you."

"Why? I'll just get them muddy on the way back to my truck."

"Oh. Right." Logic had deserted her.

"Can you get the screen door for me?"

"Sure." She reached out and opened it.

He shouldered his way through and set her down. He wasn't even puffing.

She was the one struggling to breathe. "You're stronger than I thought."

"Requirement of being a firefighter. I need that strength to handle the fire hose or carry a victim out of a building."

"Well, thank you for keeping me out of the mud."

"You're welcome."

She opened the door. "Okay, I'm here, safe and sound. You got me through the shock of seeing what the fire did to my forest and you carried me through the mud. I'm extremely grateful that you drove over with me. I should let you go back home, though."

He smiled. "Trying to get rid of me?"

"No! I'm just—"

"Being considerate. I know. I was teasing you. But before I leave there's something I wanted to talk to you about."

"What?"

"I spent a fair amount of time on your roof Saturday night and it's not in very good—"

"I know. It needs to be replaced."

"Sure does."

"Edward and I had it on the list ever since we moved in, but...you know how that goes. We procrastinated."

"I understand, but you're to the critical stage. I'd recommend replacing it with galvanized tin."

"You're right that it needs to be done. I'll call Paladin Construction first thing tomorrow."

"See, that might not work. Greg's backed up with folks wanting projects finished before the first snow."

"But—"

"I could do it."

"Oh, I couldn't ask that of you."

"You didn't. I'm offering. I wouldn't push except it's a safety issue. Those shingles look like the ones I remember from when I was here as a kid. I'm guessing the roof's at least twenty years old."

"That sounds right. The home inspector said it needed to be replaced, so the Campbells knocked down the price. We just never put on that new roof."

"After I tramped around on it all night putting out hotspots, it's really compromised. I doubt it'll hold up under a heavy snowfall."

She took a deep breath. "Then I'd be looking at a much bigger mess. And expense."

"That's the way I see it. Better to handle it now. If I measured while I'm here and got the supplies ordered, they'd probably arrive by

Friday. I could have a new roof for you this weekend."

She gazed at him. "I'd be crazy to turn down a generous offer like that. Okay. Thank you."

"Oh, and one other thing. Do you have a snow shovel?"

"In the laundry room." She grinned, thinking he was making a joke. "Have you seen a few flakes?"

"Not since last night when Cody did his spoon trick and Ryker juggled dessert plates. But if you'll fetch the shovel, I'll clear the mud from your walk before it hardens."

"Wow, I never would have thought to do that. Thank you!"

"My pleasure." He swooped in and gave her a quick kiss on the mouth.

"Hey."

"Just a tiny welcome home kiss. I'll stay here while you get the snow shovel."

She barreled into the house but paused halfway to the laundry room to catch her breath. There was nothing *little* about that kiss and he damn well knew it. No one except Edward had ever kissed her like that.

The connection had been minimal, almost not worth mentioning. So why did her lips tingle? Why was the blood pounding through her as if she'd run a foot race?

"Can't you find it?"

Whoops. Caught having a meltdown. "Be right there!" She hurried toward the laundry room.

"Are you okay?"

"Yep! Just got distracted for a minute!"

She grabbed the snow shovel and returned to the porch. "It really is a good thing you thought of this."

"Goes with the territory. Fire hoses turn dirt into mud. Can't be helped."

"Guess not." She couldn't stop looking at his mouth. His full lower lip pressing against hers had been a sensual treat. Considering the short duration of that contact, it was a wonder she could replay it in such vivid detail.

"I shouldn't have kissed you. Now you're upset."

Although her cheeks grew warm, she met his gaze. "I'm not upset."

"Are you sure? You took forever to get the shovel and you're staring at my mouth. I think I threw you off your game. If I did, I'm sorry. Sometimes I act on impulse. It's not always a good thing."

"It's a wonderful thing. I wish I could be more spontaneous, but I'm hardly ever impulsive."

"You came to my room last night."

"Not a snap decision. I debated that for hours."

"Honestly?"

"Oh, yeah. When I made that *you have no idea* comment at dinner, I was feeling reckless and giddy, which is so not like me. Then I saw how it affected you. It was irresponsible of me to say it and I don't know why I did."

"Impulse."

She groaned. "I walked right into that one, didn't I?"

"I'm not trying to match wits with you. I have a feeling I'd lose. But I don't think you're as uptight as you claim."

"Yes, I am. A more relaxed person would think nothing of that little peck you gave me. But I can't let it go. I never expected to be kissed again. True, it wasn't much of a kiss, but—"

"Hey!"

"That's not a judgment. If you'd turned it into something hotter I really would have freaked out."

"I don't want that."

She gazed at him. "What do you want?"

"Whatever you're willing to give me." He took the shovel and left.

8

Trevor scraped away the worst of the mud and leaned the shovel against the porch steps. Then he pulled his ladder out of his truck and climbed up on Olivia's roof.

After all the hours he'd spent up here the night of the fire, he knew the layout by heart. But he took his time and made sure the measurements were accurate. On his first day with Paladin Construction, Greg had taught him the cardinal rule of any project—measure twice, cut once.

From up here, the forest looked even worse than from the ground. The large swaths of missing trees stretched farther than he'd realized when he'd left yesterday. Blackened earth circled her house like a funeral wreath.

He wouldn't mention any of that to her. If the view from the ground had brought tears, this one could make her sob. He didn't much like looking at it, either. A couple of his friends had gone into the USFS. Wildfires always hit them hard, too.

After finishing his measurements, he climbed down and stowed his ladder. He needed one more thing from her. He smiled. One more thing for the roof. Dozens of things that weren't roof-related. Things that might never happen, but he could dream.

He tapped on her door.

She opened it immediately and her face was flushed, as if seeing him stirred her blood.

He hoped it did. "Hey, sorry to bother you again, but I need to ask about—"

"Color, right?"

"Right."

"I've been looking on my computer while you tromped around up there. I don't know what choices you'll have, but I'd like to have forest green or the nearest thing to it if that's possible."

"Should be, but what's your second choice?"

"Dark brown. The main thing I want is to have the roof blend in, not stand out."

"I should be able to order forest green. I'd better leave now so I'll make it to Bozeman before the roofing supply place closes. Ordering today gives us a better chance the roof panels will come in before the weekend."

"Then I'd better let you get going."

"I will." He started to leave and paused. "One other thing. Are you okay with me using your horse trailer to haul the materials when they come in?"

"Absolutely. Good idea."

"If I could drop the trailer off here on my way back instead of taking it to the ranch that would be more efficient. It'll be sometime after supper Thursday or Friday, most likely."

"Sure. Makes perfect sense."

"I wouldn't have to interrupt your evening. I could just unhitch the trailer and leave."

"That's silly. I'll want to see what you got."

"All righty, then. I'll let you know when the order comes in." He touched the brim of his hat and turned to go.

"Thank you, Trevor. This is huge."

He glanced back at her. "You're most welcome." He liked the way she was looking at him. Gave him a sliver of hope.

The following day, he used his lunch break to order a dumpster delivered to her place. He sent her a short text letting her know. She acknowledged the message with a brief *Thank you.*

On Wednesday night, he found out from his mom that Olivia had made a trip to the ranch that afternoon to return the clothes she'd borrowed. His mom mentioned that Olivia had come by right after lunch and had spent some time with Bonnie and Clyde.

Maybe she hadn't deliberately timed it so that she'd miss him. By four-thirty he was usually home, but coming later might not have fit into her schedule. He'd never asked what night she went to kickboxing. But knowing she'd been at the ranch and he hadn't bugged him.

He waited impatiently for a confirmation that the roofing materials had arrived. The order was a no-show on Thursday, damn it. If it didn't come Friday, then he'd...what? Dream up some bogus prep work just so he could drive over there?

No. She was smart, and even if she didn't know diddly about construction, she'd recognize busy work when she saw it. He wanted to preserve some small part of his dignity.

The call came on his lunch break Friday. His order was in and he had until six to pick it up. He texted Olivia that he'd be dropping off the trailer at her house around seven.

He checked his phone several times during the afternoon but she hadn't replied. Finally, after he'd picked up the trailer and before he headed to Bozeman, he looked again.

She'd texted back. *Sorry I didn't respond. Had client appointments this afternoon. I'll listen for your truck. I want to see what color you got.*

He liked that she didn't use shortcuts for words like *you*. He didn't, either. All his friends did, but he liked typing the whole thing. The other way looked like code and he'd never been a fan of deciphering messages.

But all that was extraneous to the main point. *Olivia wanted to see him.* Well, to be brutally honest, she wanted to see what color her roof would be. If that was the carrot he had to hold out, so be it.

When he pulled in a little after seven, sunset washed the sky with Eros pink. Light glowed in the windows of her house, taking his attention away from the blackened earth surrounding it. Coming home to a woman at the end of the day could be like this.

The concept had more appeal than it would have a year ago, maybe because now he was the only McGavin who wasn't in a committed relationship. Except his mom, of course, and she wasn't looking for one. He hadn't found the right time to ask if she'd ever thought about it.

He pulled the truck near the house. The lack of landscaping made that easy. His mom and her friends in the Whine and Cheese Club had offered to help Olivia plant some frost-hardy plants before the snow came. But they'd decided to wait until he'd finished the roof before implementing that plan.

She came down the porch steps at the same moment he climbed out of the truck. His heart rate jacked up just watching her walk toward him. Was that a smile? In the fading light, he couldn't be positive.

She'd created a new style for her hair. Instead of holding it back with a clip, she'd wound it on top of her head. Sexy as hell, too.

"Your hair's different."

She flushed. "I've been scrubbing the house. Even with the windows closed, ash got in. I'm taking it one room at a time."

"I like it." Piling her hair on top of her head emphasized the graceful curve of her neck.

"Thanks." She gestured toward the trailer as if eager to change the subject. "What color did you get?"

"Forest green."

"Great! Can I see?"

"Sure." He walked to the back of the horse trailer and opened it so they could get to the cartons of roofing. When he'd picked up the order in Bozeman, he'd cut out a small section of one carton with his pocket knife to confirm the order was correct.

Leaning in, she peeled back the cardboard a little more. "Sure looks like the right color."

"It's hard to see, though. I'll get my flashlight." He jogged to his truck and grabbed the one he kept in the cab. When he got back, she'd pulled away more of the cardboard. He directed the flashlight beam on the exposed metal.

"Thanks. That helps." She ran her fingers over it. "I'm glad it's a matte finish. I was afraid it would be shiny, and matte looks so much richer. This will be beautiful."

"Hope so."

"It will be, Trevor. I can't wait to see how it looks when it's finished. Thank you."

He was so close to kissing her right now it wasn't funny. "You're welcome. Glad they had the color you wanted."

"Me, too."

"I should probably unhook the trailer and be on my way, then." He switched off the flashlight.

"Have you had dinner, yet?"

"I figured I'd eat when I got home."

"I've made spaghetti sauce but I haven't cooked the pasta. I have enough if you'd like to stay."

Take it easy, McGavin. "Probably shouldn't." Had she held off on dinner because she'd planned to invite him? Things were looking up if that was the case. But he needed clarification. "Is Kendra expecting you?"

"It's not that."

"What, then?"

"I guess I need to know why you're inviting me to dinner."

Her gaze was direct. "You're going to be working here all weekend, correct?"

"That's the plan."

"Then I want to invite you to dinner as a thank-you."

He was willing to go with that. "Then I accept."

* * *

Olivia hadn't examined all her reasons for inviting Trevor to dinner. She'd known she would when she chose to make an extra-large batch of spaghetti sauce. But why do it?

On the surface, it was a nice gesture if she'd made it out of gratitude, which was the reason she'd given. But that wasn't her only motivation. She liked being with him. Life was more fun when he was around.

She helped by holding the flashlight while he unhitched the trailer and then she walked with him to the house. "Do you want wine or beer with your meal?"

He opened the screen door for her. "Neither, thanks. I'm on call. But you go ahead."

"I'm fine with water." Might be better. Alcohol would lower her inhibitions and she certainly didn't need *that*.

He followed her into the house. "Is that your diffuser or chocolate chip cookies I smell?"

"Cookies. I gave the diffuser a rest today and baked cookies, instead. I needed to replace the ones I made the night of the fire. They tasted like smoke. Do you like cookies?"

"Yep. And chocolate chip is my favorite."

"Good. Then we'll have them for dessert." Taking a calming breath, she walked into the kitchen. "Would you be willing to make the salad?"

"Absolutely. But I need to wash up, first." Walking over to the sink, he unsnapped his cuffs and rolled back his sleeves.

It was a perfectly ordinary task. It shouldn't get her hot. But as he pumped liquid soap into his palm, the muscles in his tanned forearm flexed. When he lathered up, she got lathered up, too.

Turning away, she pulled the salad fixings from the fridge and set them on the counter. "There you go."

He cupped the tomato in his hand. "Sliced, diced or wedges?" The way he gently cradled it shouldn't be sexy, either.

But it was. "Wedges." Her nipples tightened.

"Good." He ran the tomato under the faucet. "My choice, too." Then he rinsed the lettuce and patted it dry with a paper towel.

Tension curled in her stomach. There was no reason for it. He was making *salad*, for God's sake. But a broad-shouldered, lean-hipped cowboy standing at her counter expertly tearing up leafy greens inspired X-rated ideas.

She had to stop watching him. Surely there was something she was supposed to be doing if she could just remember what it—oh, yeah, start the water for the pasta. Grabbing a pot, she filled it, put it on a burner and turned the heat on.

If she set the table that would get her out of the kitchen and into the dining room. Except he was standing in front of the silverware drawer. Okay, she'd put out the pasta bowls and napkins.

Her dining table was oval, also dark wood, Edward's choice. She hadn't minded for the dining table, though. It wasn't like she would sleep on it.

Her pulse was going way too fast as she arranged the napkins with one on the end and one on the side the way she and Edward used to eat here. Then she switched the one on the end to the opposite side so there'd be no knee touching.

She placed a pasta bowl next to each napkin. Why did that look so strange? *Because you dish the spaghetti in the kitchen, doofus. Take the bowls back.*

"Your water's boiling! Want me to do anything?"

She clapped a hand over her mouth and choked back a laugh. The water wasn't the only thing boiling. As for what he could do about it....

"Olivia? You okay in there?"

She cleared her throat. "Fine! Just getting the—" What the hell was she getting in here? She glanced around. "The napkin rings! Found them! Pesky little devils." She carried the pasta bowls back into the kitchen and hoped he wouldn't notice that she was bringing back the very dishes she'd carried into the dining room.

He glanced at her. "I turned down the heat and added the pasta. It may look like I made a lot but I'm hungry. It won't go to waste, I promise."

"Thanks for doing that. You obviously know your way around a kitchen."

"Mom started us young. She wanted us to be totally self-sufficient. I think it was partly because we were down to one parent and she didn't want us to be helpless if something happened to her."

"I can see why she'd think that way." He hadn't lost one sliver of sex appeal while she'd been having a tiny meltdown in the dining room. If anything, he'd added some by taking charge of the pasta.

This was a man who'd bring her breakfast in bed and then make love to her after she ate it.

"Is this enough salad?" He tipped the bowl so she could see.

"You tell me. I can handle about a third of that."

"And I can take the rest. Are we ready, then?"

"I do believe we are."

He helped her dish up the meal and carry it to the table. Then he held her chair before walking around to take his seat. While she was a hot mess, he appeared completely at ease. He complimented her on the sauce and expertly twirled the noodles on his fork.

She, on the other hand, was so hyperaware of him that she couldn't manage the noodles without slurping and barely tasted the food. Maybe if she mirrored his body language, her brain would get the message to relax.

For the next few minutes, whenever he leaned forward, so did she. When he settled back in his chair, she did the same. The strategy helped. Adopting his rhythm settled her, and concentrating on it kept her from focusing on how great he looked sitting across the table.

She could almost ignore the slight bristle on his chin that transformed him into a dashing rogue. Or the gentle rise and fall of his chest that made her want to lay her palm over his beating heart. Or the fullness of his lower lip as he pressed it against the rim of his water glass.

He glanced across the table. "You said you were in math club. Is that why you decided to be an accountant? You like math?"

"I do, but mostly I like helping others understand it. Everyone in our club tutored kids having trouble. Now I help my clients understand taxes, which is kind of the same as tutoring." She laughed. "Although now they pay me for it."

"Why didn't you become a math teacher?"

"Thought about it. But most school teachers work for someone else, someone who sets your hours and determines your paycheck."

He nodded. "I get that. I've considered going out on my own for that very reason."

She copied his nod. "I love being my own boss. But there's no guarantee of success, no guaranteed salary."

"Did you worry about failing?"

"Honestly? No."

"I'm not surprised. You're focused and you know your strengths." He leaned forward.

And my weaknesses. She leaned forward at the same angle. "Hope so."

He studied her for several seconds. "Tell me, if I reached over and stroked your arm right now, would you reach over and stroke mine?"

Busted. Her cheeks warmed. "Uh, no."

"How long have you been copying every move I made?"

"A while."

"How come?"

"You're so mellow about hanging out with me. I thought if I did whatever you did, I might get more mellow, too."

"Has it worked?"

"Sort of." She gestured to her empty pasta bowl and a few pieces of lettuce clinging to her salad plate. "I made it through dinner without jumping your bones and demanding multiple orgasms."

His startled laughter was loud in the quiet dining room.

She stared at him, shocked at herself. "I did *not* say that. Some alien took over my body and made those words come out of my mouth."

"Or maybe you've tuned into my impulsive behavior."

"I don't think it works that way."

"Who knows? It might." He studied her, clearly amused. "I can't believe I didn't notice you doing the mirroring trick."

"It's subtle."

"Not that subtle." Heat flickered in his gaze. "Then again, my package demanded a lot of my attention. It's not easy making polite conversation while I'm calculating the weight-bearing capabilities of this table."

"Why would you do that?"

"Just trying to decide if it would hold us both."

"Trevor!" She pressed her hands to her cheeks.

"You didn't think of it?"

"*No.*"

"Not even once?"

"Of course not! I've never—" She stopped herself, but it was too late.

His expression softened. "Nothing wrong with that."

"You must think I'm boring."

"You must think I'm deranged."

Heart pounding, she held his gaze. "No, I think you're unbelievably exciting. And I'd appreciate it very much if you'd walk out the door and get in your truck. I'll…save the cookies for tomorrow."

"What about the dishes?"

"I'll do them."

He hesitated for one electric moment.

Her resistance was gone. If he made a move, she was toast.

Instead he sighed and pushed away from the table. "Okay." His smile was tinged with regret. "I'll be here first thing in the morning. Thanks for a great dinner." He left without a backward glance.

9

Knowing that Olivia believed in the importance of love in a sexual relationship, Trevor had expected the evening to end exactly the way it had. She'd surprised him a few times tonight, but the conclusion was still the same. She didn't plan to act on her urges.

His mom was on the couch with a book when he walked in the ranch house. She had a small fire going.

"Hey, Mom. Good book?"

"Oh, yeah." She put a bookmark between the pages and closed it. "Highlanders make terrific heroes. Did you eat?"

"Olivia fed me spaghetti." He took a seat in one of the easy chairs.

"That sounds messy."

"Not literally. Geez."

"It's a reasonable assumption. I've seen how she looks at you. And how you look at her, for that matter."

"Well, it's not going anywhere."

"Why not?"

"She needs to be in love to get physical and her heart belongs to Edward."

His mom digested that for a moment. "Then why is she looking at you like you're the last piece of fudge on the plate?"

"She can't help herself."

His mom started laughing and couldn't seem to stop.

"It's the truth!"

She waved her hand in front of her face and kept laughing.

He rolled his eyes. "While you get a grip, I'm gonna fetch myself a root beer. Want one?"

Eyes brimming, she shook her head.

By the time he came back with his root beer, she was still smiling, but the total crackup seemed to be over.

She cleared her throat. "Thank you for that. Best laugh I've had all week."

"Glad I could help out." He took a swig from the bottle.

"So let me get this straight. She's wildly attracted to you but she doesn't want to do anything about it?"

"Exactly. She can't see herself having sex without love and Edward was the love of her life."

"I knew she felt that way after he died but when she seemed interested in you, I thought she might be modifying her stance."

"Nope." He rested the bottle on his knee and contemplated his mom. She loved those highlander books. She'd married a Scotsman and there had been no one since. "Maybe she never will."

"Maybe not, but it's kind of a shame since she likes you so much. I'm not saying you're meant for each other or anything, but I can see how you two might get along well."

"So can I, but she gave Edward her heart. End of story." He paused. *Oh, what the hell.* He plunged in. "Is that how you feel?"

His mom blinked. "About what?"

"Your heart. And Dad."

"Since I'm not dating, it's never come up."

"Is that *why* you're not dating? Because your heart is spoken for?"

In the silence that followed, her expression was impossible to read. The only sound was the pop and crackle of the fire. "This is getting deep," she said at last. "I'll take that root beer, after all."

He set his on an end table and stood. "I'll get it."

"I'll stoke the fire."

As he entered the kitchen, he was hit with misgivings. Maybe he shouldn't have brought up the subject. He grabbed a root beer from the fridge, twisted off the cap and tossed it in the trash. But he wanted some answers.

He'd bet his brothers did, too, now that they were all happily paired up and she was still alone. Did she prefer it that way or not? Might be nice to know for sure.

He returned and handed her the bottle. "I hope I didn't upset you."

"I'm not upset. Startled, but not upset." She hoisted the bottle. "Thanks."

He smiled. "Anytime."

She sipped her root beer and propped her bare feet on the couch. "Let me say up front that I consider your dad my soulmate. We fell in love when we were young and the connection was magical."

"I like hearing that."

"It's very true. When you said that Olivia ogles you because she can't help it, I laughed because I was the same with your dad. He knew it and he would have responded just like you did."

"I wish I'd known him."

"You do, in a way. Watch Ryker when he's totally focused on a task. Ian was like that. Zane's empathy for those raptors is so like your dad, too. Bryce has his musical ability and you have his knack for fixing things. Cody has his winning personality."

"He sounds amazing."

"He was. I see him in every one of you boys. Physically, because he had those broad shoulders and narrow hips, but emotionally, too. He was a good man. I wish he'd lived."

His throat tightened. "If this is too hard for you to talk about, then—"

"It's not. Is it too hard for you to hear?"

"No. I want to hear it. I'm probably not the only one. I know for a fact Bryce wonders if you'd ever want another man in your life."

"Cody asked me about it once, too. I think he was ready to sign me up for online dating."

"That sounds like him. I can't picture it for you, though."

"I can't either." She stared into the fire. "I loved your dad and I love my memories of him. You boys are constant reminders, which is nice. So often a look, a gesture, a certain way you stand, reminds me of him. Because of that, he's with me all the time."

"Then maybe that's enough."

She glanced at him. "It certainly could be. If that's how things work out, I'm fine with it. I had him and now I have you. That's plenty."

"What do you mean, *if that's how things work out*? Have you imagined something different?"

"Not specifically. Here's the deal. I don't need a man in my life. I have the five of you and even if I didn't, I still wouldn't need a token male on the premises."

He grinned. "This is sounding like some of the conversations I've overheard when I was bartending for the Whine and Cheese Club."

"Oh, yeah, we all took the pledge. Judy and Christine have husbands, but they've promised if that situation ever changes, they won't immediately hunt for a replacement. We made them sign in blood."

"Blood? Really?"

"Okay, taco sauce. We were drinking margaritas at the time. But it's binding. We put the documents in Jo's safe deposit box at the bank."

"Speaking of Aunt Jo, she doesn't seem interested in dating, either."

"She's not. And although Deidre's enjoying her time with Jim, she's not talking about making it legal. Neither is he."

"Which brings us back to you. And your *if that's how it works out* statement. Sounds like a dodge to me."

She chuckled. "You're persistent, you know that?"

"I do know that. I've been accused of it more times than I can count. And recently, too."

"By Olivia?"

"As a matter of fact. But let's not get off track, here. We're talking about you, not me."

"I have a feeling there's a connection."

"Maybe."

"I'm no dummy, Trevor. Olivia's a widow and so am I. I haven't dated and she's determined not to date even though she is itching to get her hands on you."

"I wouldn't go that far."

"You know she is. And you're blushing."

"It's the heat from the fire."

"Speaking of fires, aren't you on call tonight?"

"Yep. Got my phone in my pocket." He leaned back in his chair and stretched his legs out in front of him. He was ready to shift the focus of this conversation. "Let's create a scenario. Say a handsome guy in his mid-to-late forties blew into town."

"Is he a cowboy?"

"Do you want him to be?"

"Of course I do. Riding and horses are my life. And you boys." She took a swallow of her root beer. "I'm not hooking up with some greenhorn who insists on group singalongs during a trail ride."

"Someone did that?"

"Last weekend. I thought for sure Zane was going to gag him with a bandana."

"No greenhorns, then. Let's say a handsome, forty-something cowboy rides into town."

"On a horse? Nobody does that anymore."

"He rides in on his Harley. How do you feel about motorcycles?"

"I don't know. Never been on one. Have you?"

"A few times. It's fun. Excuse me a minute. The fire needs tending." Levering himself from the easy chair, he went over, crouched by the hearth and used the tongs to rearrange what was left of the wood. He added one more log.

It never failed to amaze him that this cheerful blaze, if turned loose instead of being caged in this fireplace, could destroy the better part of an alpine forest, especially if the forest hadn't been managed well. After working with ENFD for the past couple of months, he'd never again underestimate the power of fire.

By the time he settled back in his chair, he had more info on the Harley-riding cowboy. "He has a mustache."

"Who does?"

"Your cowboy. Are you okay with that?"

"I have no idea. I've never kissed a man with a mustache. Why does he have to have one?"

"I dunno. That's just how I see him. He's kind, generous, and very attracted to you."

"Does he have an income? I'm not getting involved with a deadbeat."

"He has an income. I'm just not sure what he does yet."

"Well, get back to me on that, because it's important."

"Let's just say he has a decent income. Would you go out with him?"

She gazed at him without speaking.

"Yes or no? Is Dad your one and only or would you consider getting to know someone new?"

She opened her mouth. "I think—"

His phone chimed. The station.

"You have to go."

"I do. House fire." He stood and dug his keys from his jeans pocket. "We'll finish this discussion later."

"Sure." She got up and gave him a tight hug. "Take care of yourself."

He hugged her back. "Always." He headed out to his truck. He liked it better when she didn't know he was going off to a fire. She worried. But it couldn't be helped tonight.

The timing had been lousy, cutting off their discussion right when she'd been about to reveal whether she'd date this mythical guy he'd dreamed up. She'd played along with his little game, though. She wasn't totally opposed to the idea.

But that was after twenty-six years. Olivia had only been a widow for three. On the other hand, Olivia didn't have five young boys to raise. In that case, three years might be enough.

* * *

Hours later, Trevor stumbled into the house, set his alarm and fell into bed without showering or changing clothes. He lay awake for a little while as adrenaline coursed through his system. They'd saved the dwelling, but more important, they'd saved the people, their two dogs and their cat.

The cat had been a challenge because she'd hidden under a bed in the kids' room. Trevor had spied her under there and by some miracle had coaxed her out. The two kids had gone a little crazy when he'd climbed out of the second story with the calico snuggled against his turnout.

He and his buddies had celebrated a "good" fire when they'd made it back to the station. A good fire, as he'd learned, meant no creature had been killed, either animal or human. The wildfire near Olivia's house wouldn't qualify. While the forest dwellers who could run, crawl or fly away had escaped, the rest had been SOL.

It seemed his alarm chimed only seconds after he'd fallen asleep. He managed a quick shower, drank a cup of coffee from the pot his mom had left for him in the kitchen and took a couple of pieces of peanut butter toast when he headed out.

Fortunately, he'd spend the day pulling off shingles and the pitch of her roof wasn't steep. The prep work wouldn't require much thought or precision.

Just like the night before, she came out when he drove up. She peered at him as he climbed out of the truck. "Are you okay?"

"I'm fine. Why?"

"You didn't shave."

He rubbed his chin. Sure enough. "Had a house fire last night."

"Is everyone okay?"

"They are. We contained it with only minor damage. Everyone got out safely."

"Good, but Trevor, you look dead on your feet. Maybe you should go home and get some rest instead of tackling this today."

"I appreciate your concern, but I checked my weather app while I had my coffee and there's a storm front moving in early next week. I need to get on this."

Her gaze searched his. "Okay. What can I do?"

"Make me some more coffee, if you wouldn't mind. One cup isn't going to hold me."

"I'm on it. Have you had anything to eat?"

"Peanut butter toast."

"Then plan to take a break at ten. I'll have something more substantial for you."

"Thanks." Evidently the offer of nourishing food had given him a new burst of energy, because his weariness evaporated. Or maybe it was the woman offering that food.

"Can I help you pull off the shingles?" She said it hesitantly, as if hoping he'd refuse the offer.

He grinned at her. "Much as sharing the time with you would be great, I'd rather have you down below making coffee and fixing food. That's a chauvinistic division of labor and I apologize in advance."

She looked relieved. "No worries. I have zero experience pulling off shingles. I might hinder more than I'd help."

"Do you still have those cookies?"

"I do. In fact I'll make some more. But I'm going to insist you eat some scrambled eggs before you load up on sweets."

"I will. And thank you."

Her smile was more powerful than a jolt of caffeine. "You're welcome."

After she went inside, he propped his ladder against the house and climbed to the roof. These picturesque shingles, otherwise known as fuel, were going down.

<u>10</u>

At ten o'clock, Olivia walked out to call Trevor in for a late breakfast. His shirt hung over the side mirror of his work truck. Shading her eyes with her hand, she peered up at the slanted roof.

He was working on this side, which gave her an excellent view. His back glistened with sweat as he ripped off shingles and threw them into the dumpster below. The stirring display of male power immersed her in a big ol' vat of lust. No telling how long she stood there. Long enough for him to glance down and spy her watching him.

He heaved a shingle into the dumpster and walked to the edge of the roof.

Her stomach bottomed out. "Don't get too close!"

"I won't." Taking off his gloves, he shoved them in his back pocket. Then he pulled a bandana out of his other back pocket, took off his hat and mopped his face. "I'm a safety-first kind of guy."

"I have a touch of acrophobia. I don't like seeing anyone standing in a place they could fall from."

He took a couple of steps back up the roof. "Better?"

"Yes. Thanks." Considerate and insanely handsome. What more could a woman want? His chest glistened with sweat, too. She licked her lips, as if she could taste the salt on his skin.

"Is it break time?"

"Sure is!" She sounded as enthusiastic as a summer camp counselor. It was a wonder she could speak after drinking in the sight of all that masculinity. From this angle his shoulders looked a mile wide. And his package...damn, she should *never* focus there. Huge mistake.

"So the food's ready?"

"Whenever you are. I just need to scramble the bread and toast the eggs." Her cheeks warmed. "I meant—"

He grinned. "I know what you meant." He rubbed the bandana over his head before replacing his hat. "I'll be right down."

"I'll start the eggs." She hurried inside. She wasn't prepared to stand next to his shirtless self. If he came in bare-chested she was in big trouble.

Dealing with his bare chest today was a hundred times more arousing than when she'd met him coming from his shower in the hall of the ranch house. This time he was laboring to save her house. And she longed to express her appreciation. Oh, man, did she ever.

Her kickboxing classes were supposed to work off excess steam, but maybe it was counterproductive. She was more aware of her body than ever in her life. Her coordination had improved, too. Bottom line, she'd be way better at sex after all those workouts. She wanted to test it.

Not that she would! Good Lord. She fanned herself and took several deep breaths. Then she whisked the hell out of the eggs.

No backtracking. She'd made her case last night and Trevor had left after their spaghetti dinner. He understood her position. But if he'd noticed her staring at him on the roof, that could complicate matters.

His boots echoed on the porch and he came through the front door into the living room. "I smell cookies!"

"That's the new batch. I want you to have plenty for the weekend." She dumped the eggs in the frying pan and glanced up.

He'd put on his shirt. He hadn't fastened all the snaps, but most of them. He'd left his shirttails out. She fought the impulse to grab the front of his shirt and yank it open.

He started toward the counter where she was cooling the cookies on sheets of waxed paper. "I know what you said, but one or two won't hurt anything."

"I disagree." A devilish impulse made her step between him and the cookies. "Sweets on an empty stomach is never a good idea."

He advanced until his body nearly touched hers. "I think it's a great idea. Haven't you heard the saying *Life's short. Eat dessert first*?"

Her breathing got all wonky and her glasses steamed up. "Haven't you heard the saying *Patience is a virtue*?"

"Heard it. Never subscribed to it." Reaching around her, he snagged a cookie. "You baked these for me, right?"

"Yes, but—"

"I'm claiming one." He bit into it and closed his eyes. "Mm."

Pulse racing, she scooted away, abandoning the field. Her glasses weren't so fogged that she couldn't see him perfectly. If she spent another second watching him eat that cookie, she'd beg him to kiss her.

She flipped into hostess mode. "Coffee's made and mugs are in the cupboard above the coffeepot. Cream's in the fridge if you use it."

"I don't, but thanks." He took down a mug and poured himself some coffee. "How about you? Ready for some?"

Some what? She pressed her lips together so she wouldn't laugh. Then she cleared her throat. "Yes, thanks."

He pulled out a second mug. "Should I leave room for cream?"

"I like it black." She dished up their plates. Concentrating on simple tasks seemed to be the only thing that calmed her runaway hormones.

"So why do you have cream on hand?" He filled the mug.

"I knew you'd be here working this weekend and I couldn't remember if you used it or not."

"Hey, that was nice of you to think of me."

He had no idea how often she thought of him.

"And these cookies are amazing. Is there a secret ingredient?"

"Ghirardelli chocolate chips."

"That explains it. Primo chocolate chips."

She picked up both plates. "We're ready to eat if you—" She stared in shock at the counter. "How many cookies have you had?"

He shrugged. "I dunno. Ten or twelve. Who's counting?"

"You'll make yourself sick!"

"Haven't, yet. When I'm doing hard physical labor I can get away with eating stuff that would normally ruin my digestion. Besides, I have a cast iron stomach."

Naturally. She'd never met such a virile man. "If you say so." She handed him a plate. "I put silverware and napkins in the dining room."

"Then let's get to it." He picked up his mug in his free hand. "This looks delicious."

"You're still hungry after eating all those cookies?"

"Yes, ma'am." He gave her a wink. "Did I say that right?"

"You did." He'd said it more seductively than he'd ever know. "I can't believe you have room for breakfast."

"Oh, I do. Mom used to call me the bottomless pit." He waited for her to go into the dining room before he followed. "All of us liked to eat, but I guess I liked it more than anyone."

"Then it's a good thing I baked another batch of cookies."

"Where are the ones from last night?"

She laughed. "I'm not sure I should tell you. I need to save some for tomorrow."

"Then don't tell me. The temptation would drive me crazy. I'll make do with what's left on the counter."

She took the same seat she'd had the night before and so did he.

After he put his napkin on his lap, he rubbed his bristly chin. "This is so nice, cloth napkins and all. And me looking like a derelict."

"No, you don't. You look like a man who spent the night fighting a fire and got up early to come work on my roof. How much sleep did you get?" She picked up her fork when she figured out he was waiting for her.

"A couple of hours." He tucked into his breakfast.

"Yikes, Trevor. And you're walking around on the edge of my roof?"

He swallowed and wiped his mouth with the napkin. "Don't worry. If I start feeling tired, I'll take a little nap in my truck. Then I'll finish up. I'm about half done removing those shingles."

"You don't have to sleep in your truck."

"Where would you like me to sleep?" His tone sounded innocent but his glance wasn't.

Face hot, she braved it out and pretended she didn't understand that look. "You can use my couch if you need a nap."

"Very kind of you."

"I'm a kind person."

"I know you are." He held her gaze a moment longer before returning to his meal. "While I was up there working I got to thinking about something."

She'd just bet he did. "What?"

"This is an older home so stuff's bound to go wrong now and then. Do you mostly handle the maintenance yourself?" He took another forkful of eggs.

"If it's easy. Repairing the wall was beyond my skills. If it's plumbing or electrical, I hire someone."

"That can get pricey."

"It can. Some things, like a leaky faucet, I just let go until I have several plumbing issues to stack on one service call."

He nodded. "Makes sense. Have you ever thought of hiring a general handyman who could take care of everything?"

"I had one, but he retired and moved away. I haven't bothered to look for someone else."

"How about me?"

Her brain stalled. "I...well...I guess maybe, if you—"

"You could pay me in cookies."

"Of course I wouldn't pay you in cookies! You're a professional." And way too sexy to be her handyman.

"I'd be doing it as a friend, not a hired hand, and cookies would be awesome. I've been buying them because I have a massive cookie habit. These are a hundred times better than any I can buy."

"Why don't you just make your own?"

"Never did learn to bake, and the process doesn't interest me, to be honest. Just the product. Mom used to bake, but she doesn't do it as much now. I wouldn't suggest this except I can tell you enjoy making them and it seems like a great trade."

"How do you know I enjoy making them?"

"Because they taste so good. You must love doing it."

"Well, you're right. I do love it. The mixing, the spooning out the batter, the way it makes the kitchen smell, seeing them lined up on the counter. I used to make them all the time for…"

"Edward. It's okay. You can say that."

"It doesn't bother you?"

"Sure it does, but if I'm going to be your friend I'll have to get over being jealous. He was a major player in your life and still is, in a way."

"Are you going to be my friend?" It was an intriguing concept but she didn't think it would work.

"I'd like to. I want to work on it. Crazy as it sounds, I missed you last week."

"I missed you, too. I probably shouldn't tell you that. You might think—"

"That you've changed your mind? I know you haven't or we'd be in the bedroom right now."

She gasped. "We would not!"

"Yes, we would, and you know it. When you tried to stop me from eating the cookies, there was a moment when you wanted me, but you were fighting it. If I'd grabbed you then…but I didn't and you pulled yourself together."

She covered her face with her hands. "You see too much!"

"I see a warm, sexy woman who can't allow herself to feel those emotions. It must be tough."

"It is." She took her hands away and found the courage to look at him. "So logically I should stay far away from you. I don't want to do that, but I can't imagine how we can be just friends, either."

"We'll never know if we don't give it a shot. I could be your friendly handyman."

"Who works for cookies."

"Exactly."

<u>11</u>

Offering to be her friendly handyman was either stupid or brilliant. Only time would tell. But he wanted to find reasons to see her, be with her. If he managed that, he'd still have a chance. He hung his shirt over the side view mirror of his truck, pulled on his gloves and climbed the ladder to the roof.

A few clouds drifted overhead, which fit with the weather report he'd read on his phone earlier. He pulled it out of his pocket and checked his weather app again. Uh-oh. The prediction had changed to a sixty percent chance of rain tomorrow night. The storm was arriving early.

If that rain had come ten days ago, there might not have been a fire. But the rain was still welcome and would potentially prevent the next fire. The timing crunched him on this project, though.

He could prep the roof today but he didn't dare start the actual installation until he'd had a good night's sleep. He put in a call to Cody.

"What's up, bro?"

"Need to ask you something." A horse whinnied in the background. Sounded like

Winston, the Paint who was the biggest talker in the barn. "Good time or bad time?"

"I have a minute. The farrier's here but it looks like she has everything under control."

"If the weather app's right, we could have a storm by tomorrow night."

"I noticed that. Wondered how that would impact your project."

"I could use some help tomorrow. Is there any chance you have a few spare hours? If you could bring Faith, that would be a bonus."

"There goes the shopping trip to Bozeman."

"Shopping trip? For what?"

"Maybe a ring. But Faith's not big on it. She'd rather spend the money on new tack for Bert and Ernie. We're still in negotiations."

"Arguing?"

"I wouldn't say that, but if I tell her you need help with Olivia's roof, she'll be happy to table the discussion."

Trevor smiled. "Leave it to Faith. She's not going to follow the crowd and expect a flashy diamond. Count yourself lucky."

"Oh, I'm the luckiest guy in the world. But I feel like I should put a ring on her finger, you know? That's the way it's done. Except she wants the new tack instead, so I have a feeling we'll be buying that."

"Could you get it next weekend, then?"

"Absolutely. Those two horses will never know the difference and maybe I can work out a compromise in the meantime."

"How about a different stone, one that's not so expensive? An engagement ring doesn't have to be a diamond, does it?"

"I suppose not. She might go for that. She's not a jewelry-wearing person to begin with, and that's part of the problem. She gets excited about new tack for Bert and Ernie, though."

"Is Bert considered your horse now, or is he still Jim's horse? I'm confused about that."

"Jim and I share Bert. It all depends on whether I'm riding with Faith or Jim is. It's cozy."

"I'll bet. Listen, about tomorrow, it'll be hard work. I'll pay you guys."

"Is Olivia paying you?"

"She probably plans on it, but I can't see myself taking the money for labor. Materials, yes, but not labor. After last weekend with the fire and everything, she's like family."

"I know. I can hear it in your voice. Don't worry about paying us. We'll need to feed and muck out stalls first thing, then help Mom and Zane get organized for the trail ride that's going out at nine, but we could be over there before ten, no problem."

"Thank you."

"Hey, this is a golden opportunity. I've been wondering about the dynamic between you two. This will give me a ringside seat."

"There's no dynamic."

"Hell if there isn't."

"Seriously, there's no—"

"Gotta go. Licorice."

"Okay. Right." He disconnected. Licorice was a boarder, one who'd been spoiled rotten before she arrived at Wild Creek Ranch. His mom had suffered a broken leg because of Licorice's antics. The mare's disposition had improved, but she was still the least well-behaved animal on the ranch.

Tucking his phone away, Trevor went back to ripping out shingles. Now that he had backup tomorrow, he was confident the job would be done before the storm hit. He'd talked Olivia into this roof replacement and he couldn't leave her vulnerable to bad weather.

He paused as the truth hit him. He didn't want to leave her vulnerable to anything. Not fire or drenching rains. Not a loose board on her porch steps that she might trip on. There was a loose board that should be nailed down or replaced with one that wasn't warped. And she had a burner out on her stove and the kitchen faucet leaked.

But he'd be respectful and ask first. She was proud of managing successfully on her own after Edward had died. No one had the right to take that away from her. It was one of her qualities he admired.

And damn, the woman had courage. She'd clearly been scared to death the night she'd driven away hauling two horses behind her. She'd done it anyway because it needed doing. That might have been the moment he got hooked on Olivia Shaw.

More clouds bubbled up like gigantic soapsuds on the horizon, still white and fluffy, but they prompted him to work faster. He was almost out of shingles to tear up when the ladder rattled. Someone was coming, but who? Couldn't be Olivia, who was afraid of heights. But nobody had driven in so it had to be her.

Damned if she didn't appear at the edge of the roof wearing a backpack. "Need a cookie fix?"

"Hey! I thought you had acrophobia."

"I do, so if you'd help me the last little bit I'd very much appreciate it."

"Sure thing." He hadn't wanted her to see the decimated forest from this vantage point but he had no choice. He wasn't going to tell her to go back down after she'd climbed the ladder with cookies in her backpack. For him. Even though she was scared. That warmed his heart.

Pulling off his gloves, he tossed them down and walked over to the ladder. "Give me your hand."

She put her hand in his and then glanced at the ground and sucked in a breath.

"Don't look down. Look at me."

Her gaze found his. He focused on those big brown eyes and talked her up onto the roof. "One foot on the roof. I've got you. That's good. Now the other foot. Walk forward, toward me. Pretend you're climbing the slope of a hill. There. You're here." He folded her into his arms because it seemed like the right thing to do.

Oh, yeah, absolutely the right thing. She fit perfectly.

Gradually the tension eased from her tight muscles and she relaxed against him. "I didn't think this through." She continued to hold his gaze. "I'm up here, but eventually I have to go down."

"Not yet." He lowered his head.

"Trevor…" Her voice contained a warning.

"It's okay. I won't let it get out of hand. I have whiskers that would scrape the rust off a tailpipe."

"But—"

"Shh." Mindful of his beard and her glasses, he kissed her gently, slowly, parting her lips with his tongue but not venturing far. It wasn't the time. It might never be the time for what he really wanted.

But he'd take pleasure in this generous gift. She'd conquered her fear of heights to bring him cookies. So special.

Savoring the velvet softness of her mouth, he tasted chocolate. She'd been sampling the chips. When he dipped his tongue a little deeper, her breathing changed and a slight tremor ran through her body.

He wanted to soothe her, not freak her out. Her warmth tempted him to draw her closer, but he decided against it.

Instead he pulled back before the inevitable happened and he tapped into the passion he held firmly in check. Standing on a pitched roof wasn't the place for it and she clearly wasn't ready for more than this.

Cheeks flushed and lips moist, she glanced up at him. "Great distraction." She took a shaky breath. "I forgot where I was."

"Well, that's good, then."

"Yeah." Her gaze searched his.

If she kept looking at him with those big brown eyes he was liable to kiss her again and that would be a mistake. He cleared his throat.

"Are you telling me you have cookies in that backpack?"

"I do."

"Then come sit on the peak of the roof. You'll feel more stable there." He held her hand as she made her way up.

She sucked in air. "This is scary. I keep thinking I'll slide back down."

"You won't. I've got you."

"Good thing my roof isn't as steep as some around here. The one at Wild Creek Ranch is like a playground slide."

"Because we have an attic. You just have a crawl space."

"Whatever. I won't be climbing Kendra's roof. Should I sit with both legs on one side or straddle the top like I'm riding a horse?"

"Whichever makes you feel steadier."

"I'll do the straddle thing." Her fingers tightened. "Don't let go of me yet."

"I won't." He kept his grip firm as she sat down.

"Okay. You can let go."

Too bad. He'd enjoyed every minute of that. But he released her hand and sat facing her.

She slipped out of the backpack straps and settled the pack in front of her. "I also brought a thermos of coffee."

"Did you bring two mugs?"

"I sure did. It's my first time on this roof and that deserves a celebration." But before she unzipped the pack, she glanced around at the forest. Her eyes widened and she gulped. "Oh. Oh, dear."

"I didn't want you to see it from up here."

"It looks so much worse."

"I know."

She gazed at the missing chunks of forest and the charred trees that remained standing. Then she glanced at him. "Do you suppose…"

"What?"

"That this part of the forest needed a fire?" Her voice trembled slightly.

"I don't know. If so, my buddies and I did everything in our power to put it out. Maybe that went against what nature intended. But it's what we do. And your house was at risk."

"Was mine the only house in the way?"

"The only one in immediate danger."

"Would they have sent as many people and helicopters if my house and barn hadn't been here?"

"Oh, yeah. Anything this close to town would be hit with everything we've got."

"This place is pretty close, which was a selling point. I can get into town in five minutes whereas I'll bet coming from the other direction it takes you twenty."

"It does. The chief was worried about you, but he also knew if this place went, the town would be next. Good thing Ryker spied it and we could jump on it right away."

She surveyed the landscape again and took a deep breath. "This is hard to look at."

"Yes."

"But I'm glad I'm looking at it with you."

"Me, too."

Her attention swung back to him. "Now they're saying the storm will come in tomorrow night."

"I saw that. And I'm not the least surprised you checked on it, too."

"I'm an accountant. We check on everything. The report could turn out to be wrong, but—"

"I'm not taking that chance. Since I've decided not to start the installation until I get some sleep, that gives me all of one day to get this finished."

"Is that enough?"

"Not for one person. I called Cody. He and Faith will be here tomorrow morning before ten."

"That's awesome."

"With three of us working, we'll make it, no problem."

She beamed at him. "Excellent strategy. I'll bake more cookies tonight."

"They'll love that."

"And lunch. I'll provide lunch." She glowed with excitement.

"They'll love that, too."

"You know how in the olden days they had barn raising?"

"Yep." When she became animated, she transformed from pretty to beautiful. But if he said that she might think he was using flattery to get his way. Not his style.

"This feels like that, the neighbors coming to help, even if we're not exactly neighbors."

"Friends, though."

"Yes, definitely friends." She unzipped the pack, pulled out the mugs and the thermos and handed them to him. "The lion's share of the coffee is for you. I want you alert when you're walking around on the roof."

"Now that you're here, I'm very alert."

She glanced up at him. "You have that look again."

"What look?"

"The flirty look."

"Can you blame me? You're all sparkly and flushed from talking about the plan for tomorrow and it's damned attractive. On top of that, you came up here with cookies for me when heights scare you. Every time I turn around you're doing something admirable or adorable."

"So are you! Battling to save my house, using your weekend to put on a new roof—you even came over as promised even though you've had almost no sleep."

"Because I wanted to honor that promise. It was important to me." He held her gaze. "Maybe it's time to admit we really like each other."

"I do really like you."

"I really like you, too." He searched her expression for any trace of wariness and found none. "Maybe...maybe that's enough."

"Maybe." She didn't shy away. Instead she regarded him with a soft smile and a thoughtful gleam in her eyes.

He stayed quiet, let the moment stretch out as he held her gaze.

She swallowed. "Will you...will you give me some time to think about it?"

"I can do that." He could barely breathe. Somehow he'd gone from no chance to a good chance. He was determined not to mess it up.

_12_

Friends with benefits. Olivia had heard the term plenty of times and had never understood it until now. The concept lived in that gray area between having sex for the heck of it and having sex because you were deeply in love.

What if you had sex because you were strongly attracted to someone you liked and admired? Someone whose kiss made your bones melt?

She stayed on the roof until Trevor took off the last few shingles. She needed help down, but she also liked being near him. As a bonus, the longer she sat on the peak of the roof, the less scary it became.

Sitting helped. Having Trevor close by helped even more. She wasn't ready to sign up for a rock-climbing class, but she was more optimistic about conquering her fear than she'd ever been before.

Trevor heaved the last shingle in the dumpster, walked over and sat facing her again. "Have you ever figured out why you're afraid of heights?" Picking up the plastic tub of cookies, he popped the lid.

"Sure. It's very straightforward. When I was seven months old I fell down a steep flight of stairs."

"You remember that?"

"Not consciously. But I couldn't figure out why I hated ladders and stairs so I asked my mom and she reluctantly confessed that I'd taken a tumble when I was a baby."

"What were you doing roaming around on the second floor by yourself?"

"Mom didn't know I'd learned to climb out of my crib. She didn't bother with the baby gate when she put me down for a nap."

"Ouch. I guess that could have turned out a lot worse than it did."

"She feels guilty to this day. She offered to pay for therapy but I didn't take her up on it. It doesn't seem like that big a deal, although when Edward and I looked for a house here, I insisted on a single story. It limited our options."

"I love two-story houses."

"Even though the ranch only has one?"

"Yep. Don't get me wrong. I love that house. But my favorite spot as a kid was the attic. Even though it only has one tiny window and gets hotter than hell in the summer, I begged Mom to put a bedroom up there for me. Wasn't in the budget."

"Then you need to build a two-story house so you can finally have a second-floor bedroom."

"I plan to."

"I was the exact opposite from you. I begged for a room on the first floor."

"Did you get it?"

"Sure did. When I finally admitted hating the stairs and found out why, my mother was horrified that I'd been scared all that time. I think she would have built that room with her bare hands if necessary."

"Do they come out here, much?"

"They've been several times and I go see them, usually at Christmas. After Edward died they wanted me to move back to Evanston, but I'm a Westerner, now. I can't imagine living in a city again."

"I can't image living in a city, period." He shuddered. "It would be hell for me."

"Have you ever visited one?"

"Bryce and I went through several on the way to Texas and then again coming back home. I don't know how people stand the traffic."

"Now that I've been here for six years, I don't like it, either." She studied him. "Would you build your two-story house on Wild Creek Ranch property?"

"Probably not. I'd like my own land. A barn. My own horses. The ranch will always be special to me, but..."

"You want to put your own stamp on things."

"Yep."

"I can understand that. Have you figured out what the house will look like?"

"I don't have it all planned, but definitely it'll have a big rock fireplace in the living room."

"Excellent. I love the location of this house, but I was always sad there was no fireplace. What's a cold winter's night without one?"

"And where do you hang the stockings on Christmas Eve?"

"Exactly! I grew up with a nice brick one in my folks' house but that wouldn't fit here. You need something more rugged."

"I could build you one."

She smiled. "One project at a time."

"Fair enough."

She wasn't ready to tell him that her time in this house would be limited. Assuming the state took over stewardship of the cave, the house might work as a visitor center or administrative offices, though.

He held out the tub. "You should get the last one."

"Not me. Those were for you."

"And I surely appreciate it. They got me over the hump." He ate the last cookie and tucked the container in her pack. "I'm done for the day. We can go back down."

"I can't say I'm looking forward to that part."

"Want me to carry you down? I am a firefighter, after all."

"No, thanks. I've seen videos of how firemen carry people down ladders, with their head hanging down and their ass in the air. That's not for me."

He grinned. "Just a suggestion."

"I'd like a better one, please."

"Then let me have the backpack and I'll start down first."

"And I'll still be up here?"

"You'll climb down right after me so I can steady you from below. Unless you want to go down first."

"No. No, I don't." Panic clawed at her. Sitting still with Trevor inches away was fine. Crouching at the edge of the roof while Trevor started down the ladder... Her stomach pitched. "Let's not go yet."

He gazed at her. "Waiting won't make it any easier."

"It might." Her teeth began to chatter and she clenched her jaw. Sweat popped out on her forehead. Great. He could probably see that.

He glanced at his phone. "I know what we'll do." He tapped the screen and put the phone to his ear.

"You're c-calling someone?" Talk about embarrassing. "D-don't do that. I c-can—"

"Hey, Bryce. You in the middle of anything? Perfect. Could you make a little detour to Olivia's place? Thanks, bro." He disconnected.

"You called your brother?"

"Sure. I thought he might be driving from Nicole's to the GG about now, which he is. You're not that far out of his way."

"I can't believe you called your brother."

He reached over and squeezed her knee. "That's because you can't see how white you are. And you may not have noticed, but you're shaking like a leaf. If Bryce hadn't been available, I would have gotten you down somehow, but this way you won't have to be as scared with two of us to guide you."

"This is so humiliating."

"Nah. It's just me and Bryce. My other option was calling the station."

"Okay, that w-would have been worse."

"And I hear his truck already. That's the advantage of you being near town. And here he comes."

A dusty pickup pulled in next to Trevor's work truck and Bryce climbed out wearing his all-black, Johnny Cash look.

Her panic eased a little just seeing him walking toward the house. "He must be performing tonight."

"Yep. He and Nicole will do a couple of duets when the band takes a break. It's getting to be a regular thing." Trevor stood. "Hey, buddy, thanks for coming!"

"You bet! Looks like you pulled off all those shingles."

"Sure did! Listen, Olivia climbed up here to bring me some cookies and she's a little nervous about going back down. Got some acrophobia going on. If you'll come up and steady her from below, I'll help her get situated on the ladder."

"Absolutely."

She cleared her throat. "I'm totally embarrassed about this, Bryce." But her pulse rate had slowed. These two strong cowboys wouldn't let her fall.

"Hey, don't be embarrassed. Ladders are tricky. We're not all part monkey like Trev."

"Thanks." What a sweetheart. She was so giving him a discount on his tax preparation.

She clung shamelessly to Trevor as he walked her down the incline to the ladder. He held the ladder with one hand and her with the other as she turned around, searched with her foot and connected with a rung.

"There you go," Bryce said from right below her. "Keep coming. I'm here." He put a hand on her calf.

"You got her, Bryce?" Still holding her hand, Trevor stretched out flat on his stomach for maximum reach as he kept his gaze locked with hers.

"He's got me." Olivia didn't like the idea of him lying so close to the edge. "Let go."

"Yeah, I've got her, bro. Turn loose."

Gripping the ladder with both hands, she lowered her other foot to the next rung.

"I'm right here," Bryce said. "You're doing fine."

Trevor crouched near the ladder and watched her descent. When she managed a wobbly smile, he flashed her a grin and gave her two thumbs-up.

With each step, her fear ebbed. When she was on the bottom rung, she took a deep breath and glanced over at Bryce. "I need to do it again."

He nodded. "Okay."

"You don't have to stay. I'm sure you have things that you—"

"Nothing critical. This feels important."

"Yeah, I think it is." She looked up at Trevor. "I realize I'm a pain in the ass, but I want to try it again and see if I can do it without either of you holding onto me. I'll holler if I need help."

"All righty." He stood and moved away from the ladder. "Go for it."

She climbed the ladder with no problem. That was the easy part. But when she reached the top, she hesitated.

"Focus on me." Trevor's voice was calm. "Hold onto the ladder with both hands and put one foot on the roof. Then push yourself up, step with the other foot and keep walking toward me."

Heart pounding, she followed his directions. And made it! Gasping for breath, she stood in front of him.

"Awesome." His smile bathed her in warmth. Then he lowered his voice. "I would kiss you right now, but my brother's here."

"Right." She gulped in air. "Now I have to go back down."

"You've got this."

"I hope so."

"Want a hand?"

"Just at first. Don't lie down on your stomach like before. Let me mostly do it."

"I will." True to his word, he gave her only enough support to keep her from freaking out.

Bryce called from below. "Want me to come partway?"

"No, thanks! Just hold the ladder." When she reached the ground, she gave him a hug. "Thank you for being here. Between you and Trevor, I felt secure enough to try that."

"Want to do it again?"

"Not right now." She looked up at Trevor. "I'm going to quit for today. I'll practice some more tomorrow when Cody and Faith are here."

"Sounds good." Slinging her backpack over his shoulder, he came down the ladder about three times faster than she had.

That was okay. She'd done it almost by herself and tomorrow she'd get even better.

"Cody and Faith are coming over?" Bryce pulled his keys out of his pocket. "What for?"

"Storm's due tomorrow night." Trevor handed the pack to Olivia before collapsing the ladder and leaning it against the house. "I needed backup to finish the roof before it hits."

"I could help in the morning." Bryce nudged back his hat. "What time you starting?"

Trevor laughed. "Too early for you, hotshot."

"Hey!" Bryce reared back as if highly offended. "I can rise and shine like the best of them if it's for a good cause."

"How about six?"

Bryce flinched. "Is it even light by then?"

"I'll hook up some floods so we can get an early start."

"Okay. Six it is."

"And you'd rather drink castor oil than be here at that hour."

"No, I want to help, and if that's—"

"I'm kidding." Trevor punched him lightly on the shoulder. "I'll be here around seven-thirty or eight. If you can come over sometime during the morning, I'd love to have you, but don't feel obligated. It's Saturday night at the GG. You'll be up late."

"Yeah, but I can make it over here by eight." He glanced at Olivia. "Coffee would be welcome, though."

"I'll have plenty of coffee and chocolate chip cookies."

He brightened. "Oh, well, then! Why didn't you say so in the first place? Count me in."

"And the cookies are primo," Trevor said. "I gorged on them today."

"Excellent." Bryce tugged his hat over his eyes. "Then I'll see you two in the morning. Unless either of you are coming by tonight?"

Trevor shook his head. "I have to get some shuteye. Got called to a house fire last night."

"And I'll be baking cookies," Olivia said, "but maybe tomorrow night I can make it. It's a treat to watch you and Nicole perform."

His eyes lit with happiness. "Singing together is a treat for us, too." He touched the brim of his hat. "See you soon."

"Thanks again!" she called after him.

"Anytime!" He climbed in his truck, backed around and drove away, kicking up dust in the process.

She gazed after him. "He's a good guy."

"The best."

She looked over at Trevor. "You're pretty special, yourself, letting me work on my issue with the ladder when you're probably dead on your feet."

He regarded her quietly. "Not so dead that I don't want to haul you into my arms and kiss you senseless. You have guts, lady. That turns me on."

She sucked in a quick breath and her heartbeat jumped into the red zone.

"But don't worry. I won't grab you. You want time to think."

Any words she might have said stuck in her throat.

He peered at her. "You do need time to think, right?"

"Yes." It was almost a whisper.

"That's what I thought. And I need time to sleep. But when you mentioned going to the GG tomorrow night, I had an idea. Would you like to go with me?"

"Yes." The word came out a little stronger this time.

"Good. That'll be fun. I have the next two nights off at the firehouse, which is great timing, all things considered."

"It is."

"See you at eight, then." He touched the brim of his hat the way his brother had and walked over to his truck. As he pulled on his shirt, he turned toward her. "It's really something that you just up and decided to conquer your fear of heights after all this time. You impress me."

"Ditto."

He paused, his shirt hanging open, and just looked at her. He took a step in her direction, swore softly and turned back to the truck. "See you soon." Climbing in the truck, he closed the door with a firm clunk, started the engine and put it in gear.

If she called out to him, he'd turn off the engine. She kept herself from stopping him and he drove away.

When the sound of his truck was completely gone, she went into the house. Leaving the backpack in the kitchen, she picked up the rope and the miner's hat in the laundry room.

She'd been to the cave twice this past week to check on the bats. She was no expert, but both times they'd acted as if nothing had changed. She was willing to believe they were okay.

She credited the massive effort by the local firefighters and the other crews that had come to help. The wind must have been blowing away from this grassy slope. If the smoke and ash had filtered down here, she might have found some dead bats.

Instead the underground world evidently had continued to function despite the drama above. Cool, dank air surrounded her and the steady drip of water combined with the flutter of bat wings and soft squeaks. Her hidden world. Hers and Edward's.

Last visit she'd told him about the fire. This time she focused on Trevor. "We've become friends, friends who help each other."

Leaning against the chilled rock at her back, she turned off the light on her hat. Intimate conversations were easier in the dark.

"You and I started out as friends. Remember? You quietly smothered the fire I'd accidentally started in the chem lab. I helped you write an essay on Keats that kept you from failing your senior English class."

She smiled. Edward had been a brilliant accountant and a lousy writer. "Anyway. Do you remember saying that if someone great came along, I should go for it? And I said I could never love anyone but you?"

Her chest tightened. "I still believe that. You and I were perfect for each other. But...Trevor's a nice guy. I'm not in love with him. I just like him a whole lot. And I miss having someone to hold and cuddle with. I didn't think I would, but I do. I'm considering having friendly sex with Trevor. What do you think?"

Falling silent, she let the sounds of the cave calm her. Once she let others know about this place, she'd never have it to herself again. She couldn't come down and have private talks with Edward anymore. But she had to tell someone about the caverns, because a wonder like this should be shared with others who would appreciate it.

"That's another thing, Edward. I need a person I can trust to help me decide what to do about this cave. Trevor could be that person. But before I do anything drastic, I wanted to talk it out with you. I suppose I was hoping for a sign or something. How crazy is that?"

She sat quietly, open to whatever might occur, but nothing did. Except that wasn't entirely true. The last time she'd been here to discuss Trevor, she'd been confused and uncertain. She wasn't anymore.

She let out a sigh of relief. "Thank you, sweetie. I need to go bake a whole bunch of cookies for tomorrow. I love you."

13

Trevor went to bed so early that he was awake at dawn. He was up and dressed in time to help with the chores down at the stable and grab a quick breakfast before heading off to Olivia's. Because he'd helped feed and muck out stalls, Cody and Faith figured they'd be over a little sooner than they'd expected.

When he turned down Olivia's road, a cloud of dust ahead of him meant Bryce had beat him there. He chuckled. Evidently his brother's pride was on the line. Either that or a batch of chocolate chip cookies was calling his name.

Trevor loved cookies, too. But their importance was eclipsed by the woman who came down the porch steps as he pulled into the clearing. Damn, she was gorgeous.

All that silky dark hair drove him nuts. She'd tied it back with a red ribbon that matched the red shirt she wore. Had he ever seen her in that color? Maybe not. Looked nice on her.

She gave him a wave and walked over to greet Bryce, who'd just parked his truck. She seemed happy this morning and he'd take that as a good sign. He wouldn't count his chickens, yet, but...*what the hell? Bryce was wearing a hard hat?*

Trevor pulled in next to him and climbed out. "What's with the hard hat, bro?"

Bryce gave him a shit-eating grin. "I've always wanted to wear one of these and I'll never have a better chance. Got me a tool belt, too." He reached into the truck, grabbed it and put it on. "Whatcha think?"

Olivia stood behind him, hand over her mouth, shoulders shaking in silent laughter.

Somehow Trevor managed to keep a straight face. Bryce's goofy streak had gone underground in high school when Charity had gotten ahold of him. If Nicole had restored it, good for her. "Aside from the fact you have no tools in that tool belt, you look awesome."

"I figure you'll supply me with the tools. There was a limit as to how much I'd invest for this caper. Then you like the outfit?"

"Love it. I'm waiting for you to start singing *Wichita Lineman.*"

"Bingo." Bryce clicked his tongue and pointed a finger at him. "If I'm getting up at dawn, I'm sure as hell gonna have fun doing it. I have a complete working man's playlist right up here." He tapped his hard hat.

"Then you might break into song at any moment?"

"Count on it. This roof will go on ten times faster with me singing. See if it doesn't."

"Can't wait."

Olivia surveyed the two of them. "And I thought this day would be a grind."

Bryce stuck his hands in the pockets of his tool belt. "Not if I can help it."

"I can't decide whether to offer you two coffee or not. You both seem wired already."

"I'll take coffee," Bryce said, "with a side of chocolate chip cookies, please."

"Make that two coffees with a side of cookies." Trevor eyed his brother. "And don't think Olivia will slip you more cookies because you're funny and you can sing. She's smarter than that."

"No, I'm not." She gave him a saucy look. "I'm a sucker for funny guys who can sing. Follow me, gentlemen." She walked toward the porch.

Bryce lowered his voice. "She's into you, bro. I can tell. Capitalize on it."

"How can I when you're strutting around in your tool belt claiming all the attention?"

"Strap on your own tool belt and she'll forget all about me. You have one, right?"

"Of course I have one. And a spare I could have loaned you. I hope you didn't pay a lot for yours because I hate to see you wasting your money on something you'll use once."

"Chill, Trev. I borrowed it off your boss Greg. Same with the hard hat."

"Okay, that's good. I thought they looked familiar. Hey, the joke was great. You don't have to keep wearing the hard hat, though. The tool belt will come in handy, but the hat is overkill."

"I like the hat. Nicole likes it a lot, too. I might have to buy one."

"Oh, for God's sake. I don't want to know what sexual fantasies you and Nicole—"

"No, I mean for the act."

"What act?"

"Mine and Nicole's. She has some great ideas and Mandy can make any kind of costume we ask her to."

"So you'd wear a hard hat and a tool belt to sing *Wichita Lineman*?"

"I might. It could be fun and Nicole is up for anything. I could write some working man's songs to go with the hard hat. Now that I'm with her, ideas are coming so fast I can't get them all down."

"That's great to hear. This is what you deserve, a support system for that creative brain of yours." He opened the screen door and ushered Bryce through it.

"Fortunately I'm doing the same for her." Bryce paused. "I'm glad I came today. We've both been so busy I haven't had a chance to fill you in."

"On what?"

"Our future plans. I thought maybe she wanted to write songs, too. She might, someday, but right now she's into producing a quality show we'll be proud of whether we perform at the GG or Madison Square Garden."

"The Garden?" Trevor stared at him. "You've set your sights that high?"

"Sure. Why not?"

"I thought you didn't want a career path that would take you out of Eagles Nest."

"I don't. We don't. We know our priorities. This will always be home, but if we end up going on the road—"

"Really? What about the GG?"

"That's where Mike comes in, but we won't leave until he feels solid about handling everything. We'd never be gone too long, anyway. We'll need to come back here to recharge."

"And check on the cat."

Bryce laughed. "Yeah, Jimi's still going strong. But April's made friends with him. When she found out he was crazy about catnip, she ordered the primo organic kind. She created homemade mice and that did the trick. We have the cat-sitting situation covered, too."

"Wow. It's all happening for you."

"Looks like it."

"That's exciting." Trevor gazed at his twin. "You've found the perfect match. Your…" Now he hesitated to say it because he got a twinge of jealousy whenever he did. He was working on eliminating that, but he wasn't there yet.

"Soulmate? You know what, I'm questioning that concept."

"How can you, when Mom and Dad—"

"Yeah, maybe they were, but since he died so young, where does that leave Mom?"

Trevor lowered his voice. "Which has been my point all along. If there's only one person you can be totally bonded with and that person has a fatal accident or gets a dread disease early in your relationship, then are you SOL? That's messed up."

"I agree, bro. Maybe the idea is a load of BS."

"Unless you can have more than one."

"That's not how the idea is sold, though."

"I know. And if Olivia believes—"

The front door opened and she poked her head out. "Do you guys want coffee or not? It's getting cold and your cookies are waiting." She opened the door and stepped back. "First one in the kitchen gets the cookies I took out of the oven right before you guys drove up."

Trevor almost wedged himself permanently in the doorway as he and Bryce charged through it. Shades of their childhood. In the end, he backed off and gave Bryce first dibs on the cookies.

Olivia had agreed to go out with him tonight. If that worked out well, he might soon have all the warm cookies and hot kisses he could handle. That made him a lucky guy. Maybe he should stop worrying about this soulmate stuff and enjoy the moment.

* * *

Once Trevor and Bryce had their coffee and cookies, they headed back outside and began hauling materials to the roof. Olivia volunteered to bring them any small thing, like the cell phone Bryce had left in his truck.

She wanted practice climbing the ladder and it got easier every time. They texted her if they needed something from the ground, but she also went up several times just to check on their progress. And to hear them sing.

Bryce started off but eventually Trevor joined in. He had a great voice, too, and they harmonized as if they'd been doing it forever. When Trevor texted that he'd ripped a glove and needed the new ones in his truck, she was happy to fetch them.

Tucking the gloves in the back pocket of her jeans, she started up the ladder as Bryce began the Brooks and Dunn classic *Neon Moon*. She paused just below the roofline and waited until Trevor chimed in. The song was punctuated with the soft buzz of a cordless screwdriver as they fastened the panels in place.

She'd never paused while going up or down for fear that would make her more nervous. But they were rocking that number and she didn't want them to quit singing. They might if Trevor noticed her and came over to get the gloves.

Closing her eyes so she wouldn't be so aware of the distance to the ground, she listened. That sexy cowboy harmonizing so beautifully with Bryce was taking her out tonight. Excitement made her tingle.

Any woman who'd managed to snag Trevor's attention should have the mojo to stand poised on a ladder ten feet in the air and enjoy the view. Serenaded by the McGavin brothers, she took a breath, opened her eyes and looked around.

Her stomach didn't pitch, so maybe she'd mostly conquered this. She'd also adjusted to the changed vista so the gaps in the trees didn't bother her the way they used to, either. Something would grow there, something new.

When the song ended, she climbed the last little bit and called out to them. "Great job on *Neon Moon*!"

Bryce swept her a bow and Trevor tipped his hat. Then he put down his screwdriver and started toward her.

"I'm guessing you used to perform together."

"Years ago. We were just fooling around, though. We—"

"Hey! It was more than fooling around. We were a smash hit in elementary school and junior high. Then bozo, here, went out for baseball and broke up the act."

Trevor sighed. "You need to tell her what happened after that."

"Your pitching arm won Eagles Nest the state—"

"With your musical career."

"I landed a bunch of gigs."

"More than we ever did as a team, right?"

"Right, but—"

"Admit it. I did you a huge favor."

"Olivia, he *accidentally* did me a huge favor. It wasn't like he did me a favor on purpose. So how's the cookie supply holding up?"

"I still have more." She handed Trevor his gloves. "Want me to bring you both some?"

"That's okay." He gave her the ripped pair. "I can come down for them."

"Except I like climbing the ladder now. And I like hearing you sing. How about *Boot Scootin' Boogie*?"

He grinned. "It so happens we know that one."

"Don't start until I call out. See you in a minute."

After that she spent more time on the ladder than she did on the ground. Even if she had no reason to climb up, she did anyway.

When Faith and Cody arrived, she had the bright idea to grab her cell phone and take pictures of the four of them before Bryce had to leave. But when she climbed to the top of the ladder with her phone in hand, the guys had all stripped off their shirts. She hesitated.

Faith spotted her and walked over to the edge of the roof. "What's up?"

She leaned closer to Faith and kept her voice down. "I wanted to take pictures of everybody working, but would that be creepy?"

"Why would it be creepy?" Faith tossed her braid over her shoulder and crouched down. "Pictures would be great."

"But all three of them have their shirts off."

"And that's a problem because?"

"I don't want them to think that's why I'm doing it."

Faith's smiled. "Are you saying it isn't?"

"No. I mean, yes, they look really good, but—"

"And that should be recorded for posterity. It's not often you get three McGavins shirtless. I'm glad you thought of it." Faith turned. "Hey guys! Olivia wants to take pictures. Strike a pose."

Trevor paused, his screwdriver in one hand. "What kind of pose?"

"That's good right there." Faith turned to Olivia. "Start shooting, girlfriend."

Cody lowered a metal panel. "What do you want me to do?"

"Pick that up again and turn this way. Excellent. Bryce, grab that roll of roofing felt and look over here. Perfect. You getting all this, Olivia?"

"Yes, ma'am." Her cheeks were warm but she snapped away. "Now you get in the picture, Faith."

"Okay." She walked carefully around the panels that had been laid. "Where should I stand?"

"Let's pick her up," Cody said. "I'll take her waist and you each grab a leg."

"Hey!" She propped her hands on her hips. "Did I say you could do that?"

Cody paused. "You don't want us to?"

"Of course I do. It'll be fun. But you're supposed to ask."

"Okay. Do you want us to pick you up so it'll be a way cooler picture?"

"Yes, please!" She started laughing as they hoisted her in the air and she spread her arms wide. "Wheee! I'm a cheerleader!"

What a shot. Olivia couldn't stop smiling. "That's a keeper! Thanks!" She was also a tiny bit jealous of Faith, who had such a great relationship with those guys. With the entire McGavin family, in fact.

Later that day, when Faith came down to use the bathroom, she asked to see the pictures on Olivia's phone. "I love them!" She scrolled through them once and then went back through a second time.

"You're all so photogenic."

"Those McGavins sure are. Not an ugly one in the bunch."

"But you look great, too. Happy."

"I am happy, happier than I've ever been. I'm so glad you took pictures. The guys wouldn't think of it and I left my cell in the truck. I was afraid I'd drop it off the edge of the roof or something." She handed over the phone. "Oh, wait. Can I send them to mine?"

"Absolutely." She gave it back. "You sure are relaxed with those guys."

"I've been around men all my life so that's easy. It's women I had to learn how to deal with. But I'm getting better at it. Anyway, I should get back up there. We're almost done, which is fortunate because those clouds are moving in."

"I'm coming to watch the final stage." She followed Faith outside.

"It looks nice, if I do say so. Trev knows his stuff."

"Yes." She gazed up at the beautiful man on her new forest green roof. "Yes, he does."

"He said you're coming to the GG to party with us tonight."

"I sure am. Wouldn't miss it."

Faith gave her a warm glance. "Good."

<u>14</u>

Trevor's energy level was off the charts. After spending a day installing a new roof he should be exhausted, but his body hummed with anticipation. He rolled right over the front walkway so he could park as close to Olivia's front steps as possible.

He'd cleaned the truck's interior and the rain coming down had taken care of the exterior except for whatever mud he'd splashed up on his way here. The area at the bottom of her steps was a mud hole, but he'd anticipated that.

Pulling a wide board from behind the seat, he took it with him as he eased out of the cab and onto the walk. His boots got muddy on the way around the truck but the board would keep hers relatively clean. After laying the board across the muddy patch, he climbed the steps.

She opened the door before he could knock. "I'm ready."

His breath caught. "You sure are. Wow." Her hair flowed in ebony waves down her back and over her shoulders. Her lemon-yellow blouse was unbuttoned far enough to show some cleavage and her denim skirt only reached to mid-thigh. Her boots were short and the heel was high. Party boots.

But something was missing. "Where are your glasses?"

"I'm wearing contacts. Usually I don't bother with them but I felt like dressing up tonight." She looked him over. "Seems like you did, too. That's some fancy silver embroidery on your shirt. Did you skip the hat?"

"Left it in the truck. One less thing to get wet." He couldn't stop staring at her. "You look...delicious."

Her cheeks turned pink. "Thank you."

"Do you have a raincoat? It's coming down pretty hard."

"Right here." She'd draped it over her arm. "Just let me lock up."

He'd been too busy admiring her hair and, okay, the fit of her blouse and her sexy legs, to notice she was carrying a raincoat. And a purse.

After locking the door, she tucked her keys back inside of it and faced him. "Should we go, then?"

"Um, yes." He snapped out of an erotic daze in which he'd leaped forward in time to the moment he'd bring her back here and she'd unlock that door. "Let me help you with your coat."

She gave it to him and turned around so he could slide it up over her arms and shoulders. "Thanks." She turned back to him, tied the belt and put up the hood. "All set."

"I'll go first and get the door open. I put a board down so you'd have something to step on."

"What a nice guy!"

"Glad you think so." He ached to hold her. Did she dance? He'd never asked. But this was Nicole's night to perform, so the music would be geared to sing-alongs instead of dancing.

He opened the passenger door and went back for her, leading her quickly across the board and into the cab. He closed the door and hurried around to the driver's side. By the time he made it inside, closed the door and started the engine, his hair dripped and his shirt stuck to the upholstery.

"Why didn't you wear a raincoat?"

"Don't own one." He put the truck in gear and pulled out.

"That's hard to believe."

"I have a slicker I wear if I have to be on a horse in the rain. It's not nice enough to take on a date."

"A date. I don't think I've ever been on one before."

"Didn't you date Edward?"

"Not really. At first we were just friends hanging out. By the time it became more, we were past the dating stage."

"So we're friends, right?"

"I hope so."

"I'd definitely say we are, so maybe this doesn't count as a date."

She glanced at him. "But it's not like we're just hanging out with each other."

"True. If we were, we wouldn't be so dressed up. I'll bet if it wasn't a date you'd be wearing your glasses instead of contacts."

"Yep."

"And you would have fastened more buttons on your blouse and worn a longer skirt."

She groaned. "Is it too much?"

"God, no. I love how you look. When you came to the door I was so tempted to—" He swallowed what he'd started to say. Her outfit might mean that she'd thought about their situation and had arrived at a conclusion he'd be very happy about. But he'd be wise not make that assumption.

"Tempted to do what?"

"Never mind. I'm coming on too strong. I'll tone it down." He sure as hell didn't want to lose what ground he'd gained.

"The thing is, I like it."

"You do?"

"Your eagerness is…exciting."

"Ah." He smiled. All was not lost. "I'm still not going to finish that sentence, though."

"Maybe that's just as well." She took a breath. "Let's talk about something else."

"Like what?" He hoped she had some conversational topics because his brain was fried.

"Like my beautiful roof. It's amazing. The clouds were moving in by the time you all finished and I didn't have nearly enough time to compliment the job you did."

"I could tell you liked it, though." The image of her happy smile had warmed him during the drive back to the ranch.

"I absolutely do. The color's gorgeous and it gives the house a crisp look that's so pretty. The shingles made it shabby. I didn't realize how much they detracted from the appearance until you ripped them off and replaced them with tin."

"I have to admit it's a hundred percent better."

"A thousand percent better. Then the rain started and I got to hear it on the roof. Turns out I really like that sound."

"I'm glad."

"It's a fabulous roof, Trevor. Thank you."

He gave her a smile. "My pleasure."

"By the way, Kendra called after you left. We set up the Whine and Cheese planting party for Wednesday afternoon. She and I are going to buy everything tomorrow."

"Yeah, she mentioned something about that. Have you ever seen the Whine and Cheese ladies in action?"

"I caught their belly dancing act during the Labor Day Parade, but other than that, no, I haven't."

"You'll have a blast."

"I'm honored they want to help. I could do it myself, but—"

"Why should you? They can manage in one afternoon what would take you days working alone."

"That's what Kendra said."

"And they get such a charge out of it." He turned into the parking lot at the GG. It was packed, as usual. "Looks like the rain's let up." He found a spot and turned off the motor.

"Your shirt's still wet."

"It'll dry." He reached behind his seat. "I brought a towel to clean off my boots before we go inside."

"Is the towel clean?"

"Yes."

"Then let me have it before you wipe off your boots."

"Sorry. I should have offered it to you, first. That board didn't completely do the trick, did it?" He handed it to her.

"It's not for my boots. Lean over. I'm going to dry your hair."

Sounded like fun. He unsnapped his seat belt and turned so she could reach him. "How's that?"

"Come closer."

Now he was inches from her face. And her mouth. Her lipstick was the color of ripe peaches and she'd applied it with great care. He wasn't going to smudge it. But how he wanted to.

She rubbed the towel briskly over his head. It didn't qualify as a caress, but it was sensual. He liked it.

"Okay, that's better." She put the towel in her lap and began to finger-comb his hair into place.

Now *that* was a caress. She might deny it, but her breathing told him different. "You should probably stop doing that."

"Why?" Her voice was almost a whisper.

"Because if it's turning you on as much as it's turning me on, we'll never make it into the GG."

"You'd drive us back to my house?"

"No, we'd have sex in the front seat of this truck."

"But that's impossible. For one thing, you don't have—"

"Guess again."

She gulped. "Oh." She handed him the towel and put more distance between them. "Then I guess you'd better clean your boots."

"That was the plan." He opened his door so he'd have room to maneuver and pulled off the left one.

"Could we really do that?"

"Do what?" The mud had partially dried so he had to work at the job.

"Have sex in the parking lot?"

"Yes, ma'am. This spot isn't well lit. The people who own the vehicles on either side of us are inside having a good time. No one would know."

"It's not only that. It's the logistics."

Since his back was to her, he could allow himself a smile. Her husband hadn't had much adventure in his soul if she couldn't figure out the logistics. "It's entirely possible to manage." He put on the clean boot and took off the muddy one.

"This truck doesn't have a back seat."

"So you use the passenger seat."

"I don't see how that would work."

"But it does." The discussion was stirring him up but she wasn't backing off it so he kept going. "I'd sit on the seat and you'd climb aboard."

"Oh." She took a quick breath. "I didn't think of that."

"Because you didn't engage in teenage make-out sessions, I'll bet."

"No, but I'm guessing you did."

"For teenage boys in Eagles Nest, it was the primary motivation to get a license and a pickup. In summer, we used the truck bed, but in winter, that was too damned cold so we had sex in the cab because it had a heater."

"I've never done it in any vehicle, let alone a pickup. By the time I had sex, Edward had his own apartment."

"Then I can see why you'd have trouble imagining doing it in a two-seater truck." He put on his boot and tucked the towel behind his seat.

"I don't have trouble imagining it now." Her voice had gone from breathy to sultry.

He went still. "You want to try it?" His groin tightened.

"Not now. But sometime."

"With me?"

"You're the one who understands the logistics."

Jacked up as he was by their discussion, he had enough brain cells working to get the underlying message. He turned to her. "So you're willing to have sex with me at some point in the future?"

"Yes." She swallowed. "Yes, please. I...think it would be...wonderful."

"Ahhh." He sank back against the seat and took several deep breaths.

"Are you okay?"

"More than okay. Although I was hoping, there was no guarantee. I'm ready to drive straight back to your house, but we should make an appearance."

"More than an appearance. I love your family. I want to party with them. I probably shouldn't have asked you about having sex in the truck. That got us going down that road. My bad."

He reached over and stroked her velvety cheek with the tip of his finger. "I think there's a part of you that wants to walk on the wild side. Just a little bit."

"I think so, too."

"Then we will. Later." He leaned closer and gave her the lightest of kisses, one that wouldn't smear her lipstick. "Let's go inside. And we'll stay until you're ready to leave."

Two hours later, he had some regrets about that promise, but Olivia was blossoming. She'd never been to the Guzzling Grizzly when Nicole was performing and she loved the sing-alongs. She couldn't carry a tune in a bucket, a fact Trevor learned early because he sat next to her, but that didn't stop her from enjoying the hell out of the experience.

When he glanced over and caught her belting out a tune off-key, her face flushed with the joy of being part of the group, his heart stuttered. He'd be a selfish bastard if he denied her this because he was so eager to sink into her hot body and calm the raging fire she'd created.

Patience wasn't his long suit. He'd acknowledged that flaw years ago. But learning it for Olivia's sake made the exercise worthwhile.

He'd been surrounded by a sizeable group of supportive people all his life. Judging from what she'd said, she'd mostly had her parents. And Edward. Maybe he'd loved her without ever understanding her erotic yearnings.

Arrogant though it might be to claim that he understood those yearnings, he'd stick by that conclusion. And her.

<u>*15*</u>

Olivia nestled into the homey atmosphere of the GG and the warm acceptance of Trevor's family as if pulling a soft quilt around her heart. Safe.

She'd needed this. After Edward's death, she'd leaned on Kendra's strength but hadn't let the rest of the McGavins see her pain. She hadn't allowed herself to be part of Kendra's circle, either. She'd been too consumed by grief.

That had changed. *She* had changed. The person she'd been three years ago, even six months ago, wouldn't have sat in the GG singing at the top of her lungs. She wouldn't have exchanged hot glances with Trevor, either.

That was the biggest transformation of all. Denying herself the comfort and pleasure of a man's attentions made no sense. Edward wouldn't have wanted her to be lonely and frustrated. She got that, now.

Nicole's performance tonight was amazing and energizing. Most of the tunes were rollicking, fun songs that everyone knew. But then she announced that she'd had a request for Faith Hill's *Breathe* and she invited everyone to dance.

Trevor stood and held out his hand.

"I'm not any good."

"I don't care. Dance with me."

"Okay. I warned you." She slipped her hand into his. "Your hand's warm."

He led her toward the dance floor. "It's cool compared to other parts of me." He drew her into his arms. "I'm about to combust."

"Oh?" She gazed up at him. Those blue eyes were hot, hot, hot.

"Can you tell?" He pulled her in close and moved to the rhythm of a song that was all about making love.

"Mm-hm." Snuggled against his solid chest with his hips sliding suggestively against hers, she discovered that she wasn't such a bad dancer. All she had to do was relax and follow his lead.

"You get to decide when we head out." He rubbed the small of her back.

"Uh-huh." She molded her body to his and let her instincts take over.

His gaze darkened. "Could you…um…give me a general idea of when that might be?"

"Soon."

His voice roughened. "How soon?"

"Very soon. This is a very seductive song."

"I know. That's why I requested it."

"I wondered if it was you."

"I desperately needed to hold you. And maybe convince you it's time. I'm going crazy."

Heat curled in her belly. "We're not doing it in the truck."

"No. I'll get us back to your place."

"Even if you're going crazy?"

"Yes. Say we can leave after this song. Please. Put me out of my misery."

"We can leave after this song."

He sucked in a breath and closed his eyes. "Thank you."

"We can't just rush out of here, though. We have to say goodbye to everyone."

"We will."

And they did, but it was the shortest leave-taking she'd ever been a part of. Trevor claimed exhaustion from the roof installation but she doubted anyone believed him. He hustled her out the door and handed her quickly into the truck.

Jogging around to the driver's side, he climbed in and managed to start the engine and buckle up at the same time.

"That was efficient."

He flashed her a smile and put the truck in gear. "I'm highly motivated. And by the way, you're a terrific dancer. You were turning me on six ways to Sunday out there."

"Wasn't very difficult."

"True." He pulled out of the parking lot. "But I want to try some more of that dancing, maybe Friday night if I'm not on call. Would you be willing?"

"I would." She'd go along with just about anything he asked. She'd climbed into the front car of a rollercoaster and was ready for a thrill ride.

"Just to let you know, I'm gonna speed a little, just a few miles over, assuming the road's clear. Sunday night it usually is."

"A ticket will slow us down."

"I won't get a ticket."

And there it was, the confidence and daring that made him the sexiest man she'd ever met. Considering how fast the scenery whizzed by, he was more than a few miles over the limit, but he drove with precision and she never once was scared.

She was aroused, though. She was super aware of his hands gripping the steering wheel, his muscular thighs flexing as he worked the pedals and his chest expanding with each breath. Her lady parts tingled and her panties grew damp.

He gave her a quick glance. "Do I make you nervous going this fast?"

"No."

"Just wondered. You're staring at me so I thought you might be worried."

"I like looking at you."

He grinned. "That's good to hear."

"I've never seen you naked." Hurtling through the darkness made her say things she never would otherwise. "I want to."

"I'll be happy to grant that request." He slowed the truck as he turned down her road. "I'll take it easy going into your place. I'm not about to get stuck in the mud at this point in the evening."

"Please don't."

"Am I detecting some impatience in your voice, Olivia?"

"It's possible."

"Good. I don't want to be the only one who's desperate."

She located her keys in the bottom of her purse. "I'll hop out when we get there. Don't worry about opening my door for me."

"You realize that goes against my training."

"But you'll do it."

"Whatever gets us inside faster."

"Okay, then." She unbuckled her seatbelt as he drove up close to the porch. "See you in there." She was out of the truck before he turned off the engine.

Racing up the steps, she crossed the porch and unlocked the door.

He came up behind her. "I'm taking off my boots."

"Take off whatever you want, cowboy." She barely recognized the temptress she'd become as she walked in, left the door open and turned to face him. "I plan to." She nudged off her boots as she unbuttoned her blouse.

"Damn, woman." He unsnapped his cuffs as he came through the door and kicked it shut. His eyes glittered. "When did you turn into a tease?" Snaps popped as he yanked open his shirt.

Heart pounding, she slipped off her blouse and dropped it to the floor. "It's not a tease if I'll give you anything that strikes your fancy." She reached behind her, unhooked her bra and tossed that away, too.

"You. You strike my fancy." He sent his hat sailing toward the couch. Then he eliminated the space between them. Spanning her waist with both hands, he lifted her up. "Wrap your legs around me, lady, and hold on. I'm about to kiss the living daylights out of you."

"Please do."

With a growl, he lowered his head and claimed her mouth. It was a searing, possessive, demanding kiss. He took it deep and used his tongue to take it deeper.

She wanted that kiss with an urgency that made her tremble. Sliding her fingers through his silky hair, she gripped his head and opened to him, letting him have his way with her. Nothing mattered but the fiery emotion he ignited.

He kneaded her bottom with strong fingers and pulled her in close. She squirmed against the denim keeping her from what she wanted and rocked her hips with a moan of frustration.

He lifted his mouth a fraction from hers. His hot breath fanned her lips. "Want something?"

She gulped for air. "I want it *all*."

"That's what I like to hear."

The velvet sound of his voice stroked her to a fever pitch.

Tightening his grip, he carried her down the hall. "You left the light on."

"So you can find your way."

"Right now I could navigate this hallway blindfolded." He carried her through the doorway and lowered her to the floor.

She slid her hands over his taut six-pack and firm pecs. "Thank you for waiting for me while I thought this through."

With a groan, he cupped her face. "Thank you for saying yes." He dropped kisses on her forehead, her eyelids, her cheeks. "Thank you for letting me touch you." Holding her gaze, he brushed his thumbs over her cheeks.

"It feels good."

"That's the idea." He caressed her throat and her bare shoulders. "Let's see how this feels." Drawing her to the bed, he sat on the mattress and guided her between his knees. "Perfect." Cradling a breast in each hand, he looked up at her as he rubbed his thumbs gently over her nipples.

As they stiffened under his easy caress, sensation arrowed downward, winding the tension tighter. Her breathing quickened and she clutched his shoulders for support.

"Good?"

"Mm-hm."

"Let's try this." Leaning forward, he pulled one aching nipple into his mouth, catching it against the roof of his mouth with his tongue and rolling it back and forth.

Her breath came faster. As he began rhythmically sucking, the spring wound tighter. She dug her fingers into his broad shoulders and whimpered.

Reaching under her short skirt, he found his way past drenched silk and lace. A few strokes of his nimble fingers brought her to the edge. A few more sent her over it.

Thrusting deep, he anchored her in his firm grip as waves of pleasure swept through her trembling body. Gradually the tremors subsided and she took a shaky breath.

"Like that?" His voice rumbled in the stillness.

"It was…unexpected."

He gave her a lazy smile. "Really? You didn't expect to come tonight?"

"Oh, I did, but I thought it would happen when you threw me on the bed and went for it."

"Almost did that." He unbuttoned her denim skirt and pushed it down along with her soaked panties.

She kicked them aside. "Why didn't you?"

"It wasn't a good idea." Glancing up at her, he slipped his hand between her damp thighs. His touch was light, but fire gleamed in his eyes. "Not sure how long I'll last."

"Want to find out?"

"I surely do. Want me to throw you on the bed?"

"I sort of do. I think it would be fun."

"Okay." He moved her gently aside. "First I need to strip down for action."

"Can't wait." She moved back to get a better view.

"You've seen this part." He slipped off his shirt and let it drop. "You've seen it quite a bit today, in fact."

"Ah, but it never gets old." She reveled in the sight of his muscular chest and sculpted abdomen, the coiled strength in his arms and the inspiring breadth of his shoulders.

"Nice to hear." Unbuckling his belt, he unfastened his jeans. Before he took them off, he pulled two condoms out of his pocket. He put one packet between his teeth and tossed the other on the bedside table.

Her heart thumped in anticipation. He shoved his thumbs in the waistband of his briefs, pushed down and stepped out of jeans and briefs in one easy motion.

She sucked in a breath. She was ogling shamelessly and yet she couldn't make herself stop.

He ripped open the condom package.

"Wait."

"For what?"

"I just want to…look at you…for a minute. If that's okay."

"It's okay." He sounded tense, but also slightly amused. "Just don't take too long. Now that we're both naked, the fuse has been lit."

"I understand." Dynamite was the perfect image. His muscular calves and thighs completed the picture of masculine strength. The jut of his thick cock and the heaviness of his balls promised explosive pleasure.

She was at the top of the rollercoaster, now. No place to exit. She was in for the ride of her life. She lifted her gaze to his. "Go for it."

<u>16</u>

Trevor rolled on the condom and slipped the leash on his self-control. She'd flat out told him what she wanted. He would bring it.

Striding toward her, he dropped his shoulder, grabbed her arm and hoisted her up in a classic fireman's carry. She squealed, which was exactly the reaction he was looking for.

This maneuver was way more fun with a naked woman. The imprint of her breasts against his back was arousing as hell, not that he needed more stimulation right now.

"This isn't what I meant! Put me down!"

"How can I throw you on the bed if I don't pick you up?"

"All the blood's rushing to my head!"

"Funny, but all my blood's rushing to a different place." Too bad she didn't have a mirror in here so he could see how cute she looked with her firm little ass in the air. He reached up and lightly pinched it.

"Hey!" She pinched him back. Then she laughed.

How he loved her laughter. And just like that, he couldn't go another second without burying his cock in her hot body. He crossed to the bed and tossed her down on the mattress. It was so springy she bounced, which cracked him up and gave her the giggles again.

In no time, he was on her, wedging his hips between her thighs, laughing with her as he thrust deep. Effortlessly. A sword to its perfect sheath.

The laughter stopped and his gaze locked with hers. Yeah, this wasn't funny anymore. This was intense. Life-changing intense. He held very still while his heart galloped out of control.

Reaching up, she touched his cheek. She looked as shell-shocked as he was. Even a little scared. Hell, so was he.

But he didn't want her to be. "It's okay." Leaning down, he kissed her gently. Then he lifted his head and smiled. "It's going to be okay."

She nodded.

"Do you want me to stop?" He wasn't sure he could. The urge to complete what he'd started nearly overwhelmed him, but he had to ask. If she said yes, he'd manage. Somehow.

"No." She swallowed. "I...want this. I just didn't think it would be so...."

"Me, either." He eased back and the sweet friction made him groan. "Good."

Her tiny frown of anxiety disappeared and she wrapped her slender arms around him. "Very good."

He started slow. Something this amazing shouldn't be rushed even if his body clamored for release. With each stroke her eyes grew brighter and her cheeks turned a deeper pink.

He basked in the glow of her pleasure. When he moved a little faster, the glow increased. She wasn't scared now. She was as eager for the grand finale as he was.

And completely in sync with him. She rose to meet every thrust as if she craved the connection they made at the top of the sensual arc. He drove in a little harder and she responded by clutching his hips and urging him on.

He didn't need to ask if she was close. Her eyes told him. Her breathing told him. The undulations of her welcoming channel told him.

Reining in his climax, he concentrated on hers. Yes, there. Once more, right *there.* When her eyes widened and her spasms rolled over his eager cock, he abandoned himself to the incredible joy of sharing an orgasm. With her. With Olivia.

When it was over, when the gasps, the moans and the cries had faded away, he looked down and discovered her looking back, eyes sparkling and smile jubilant.

"That was *awesome.*"

"Not bad for a first try."

"No kidding." She cupped his cheek. "We should celebrate. I have a few cookies left. Want some?"

He laughed. "Do you even have to ask?"

Fifteen minutes later, she'd put on a bathrobe and replaced her contacts with her glasses. He'd pulled on his briefs and jeans so he could be halfway decent when they sat at her dining table eating cookies and drinking milk. A kid's snack to follow a very adult activity. He wasn't complaining.

And he liked the seating arrangement better. Before she'd made him sit across from her. Now she was at the head of the table on his right, which meant they could touch each other. He found himself touching her a lot.

She grabbed another cookie from the plate. "Thanks to you, whenever I look at this table, I think of tabletop sex."

"You're welcome."

"I wasn't actually thanking you. It's a pain in the ass to have a dining table become an erotic piece of furniture. How am I supposed to have dinner parties?"

"Do you have a lot of those?" He reached over and ran a finger over her arm because it made her shiver and her cheeks turned pink. He liked that.

"Not really." She nudged his knee under the table.

He nudged back. "Have you ever had one?"

"No."

"There you go. Problem solved."

"But what if I did have one? Then I'd be blushing all the time because I'd have erotic associations with the furniture."

"That's just wrong." Reaching under the table, he pulled her robe aside and fondled her knee.

"Yes, it is. And right now, you're making it worse." She gave him a mock glare of disapproval.

"I want to make it worse. What's the point in worrying about erotic associations when it's all in your head? If the table is already causing a problem, you might as well do the deed."

"I beg your pardon?"

He grinned. "If you're trying to cool me down, don't act prim and proper. That only makes me hotter. Especially when you're wearing your glasses."

"Are you one of those guys who gets turned on by uptight women wearing glasses?"

"Apparently. Who knew?"

"What happens if those ladies stop being uptight and start wearing contacts? Does the attraction fade?"

"Doesn't look like it."

"Yes, but can you be sure?"

"I have the perfect test. Have sex with me on this table."

She flushed, which indicated she was interested. "That's a very hard surface."

"I'll take the bottom."

She glanced at the uncovered windows looking out on the forest. "We'll be in plain view."

"Sure will. The owls and bats would see right in. They'll be scandalized."

"So we'd do this to prove whether it's my uptight vibe that has you begging for more?"

"And to give you a legitimate reason not to have dinner parties."

"Okay, I'm in." She pushed back her chair and stood. "But you'll need to grab the condom from the bedroom."

Digging in his pocket, he pulled it out and held it up.

"You've been planning this all along?"

"I swear I haven't. But I tucked it in my pocket in case of a dire emergency."

"You only brought two, right?

"More than that seemed obnoxious."

"Do you want to spend it on this?"

"Yes. Yes, I do."

She stood and dropped her robe. "Then I'm game."

Olivia standing naked in her dining room with her dark hair tumbling around her shoulders and partially covering her breasts was an arousing sight. Any man would pause and stare. Trevor was no exception.

"What?" She spread out her arms. "You've seen all this before."

"In your bedroom. And you weren't wearing your glasses."

She reached for them. "Then I'll take—"

"No, don't."

"I have to. Otherwise it's not a test. We're trying to discover if you lose interest if I become a wild woman instead of an uptight, glasses-wearing accountant. Wearing glasses during sex would taint the data."

That was the speech. That was the crazy, adorable speech that captured his heart. But instead of saying so, he merely nodded. "You're right. Ditch the glasses." It wouldn't make a damned bit of difference. Glasses or no glasses, she had him in the palm of her hand. He wasn't going to say it. Not now and maybe not ever.

Peeling off his jeans and briefs, which revealed that he was more than ready for this experiment, he started to roll on the condom.

"Let me. I want to do it. A wild woman would offer."

"Now?"

"No, when you're stretched out on the table. Are you sure you want to lie on it, though? It's extremely unyielding. I might have a camping mattress in the storage closet."

He shook his head. "We've already put too much thought into this. Ideally two people are eating at a table, get worked up, and sweep the dishes aside so they can get busy."

"Spontaneous sex."

"Pretty much."

"I've always wondered about that. What about birth control?"

He waved the condom in the air. "The guy has to be prepared."

"Are you always prepared? Because that's kind of smarmy."

"No, I'm not always prepared."

"Glad to hear it. But I'm still hung up on this table sex thing, which seems as if it could end up with spilled food, broken dishes and unplanned pregnancies."

"We don't have to worry about any of that."

She studied him for a moment. "No we don't. Let's do it."

Even though she'd killed the spontaneous factor, he would never say no to having sex with her, anytime, anywhere. He stretched out on the table. It was damned uncomfortable. In the heat of the moment, a person might not notice, but they'd talked this to death and he noticed.

Then she climbed up there, straddled him and lovingly rolled on the condom. He'd lie on a bed of nails in exchange for that privilege. Bracing her hands on his chest, she lowered her hips.

As she slowly took his cock into her warmth, he forgot about the table. Nothing mattered but the glow in her eyes, the flush on her skin, the perfect connection that was nearly…yes…now.

He bracketed her hips, holding her there, prolonging the moment when everything made sense. Such times didn't come along very often.

With a Mona Lisa smile, she slid her hands forward. Her hair swept over his hot skin as she leaned down and gave him an open-mouthed kiss. Her nipples brushed his chest. Heaven.

Lifting her head, she gazed into his eyes. "You look happy."

"So do you."

"I am. I'd forgotten what happy feels like."

"Like this. It feels exactly like this."

"It does." She kissed him again, softly. "Ready to take this happy feeling up a notch?"

"Think I can handle it?"

"Oh, yeah." Her hair caressed him as she eased back and flattened her palms against his chest. "I get the impression you can handle most anything."

She had that wrong. When it came to her, he was vulnerable as hell. Making love with her was like nothing he'd ever known. He was falling hard and fast.

She would give him her friendship. She would give him her body. But she'd made it clear she'd never give him her love. Was he strong enough to handle that? Maybe not.

<u>17</u>

For some reason, Olivia had assumed Trevor would spend the night, but after they recovered from their wild episode on the table, he held her close and murmured that he had to leave.

"I wish you could stay." The words were out before she could stop herself.

"I wish I could, too." He gave her a lingering kiss. "But I didn't plan for that and I have to get up early for work."

"That makes perfect sense." She reined in her disappointment. After blurting out that she wanted him to stay, she hesitated to ask when she'd see him again.

He pulled on his briefs and jeans. "I'm usually pretty busy during the week between Paladin and the station. But I might get an evening off. I'll text you when I know my schedule."

"Okay." Since he was getting dressed, she put on her robe and tucked her glasses in the pocket. "Murphy's Law it'll be the night of my kickboxing class, but I'm home by nine."

He smiled. "Any chance you'd be willing to skip the class just this once?"

She matched his teasing mood, which was better than acting forlorn because he was leaving. "Depends, cowboy. Give me a reason to skip the class and I will."

"I'll give you a reason." Grabbing her, he kissed her until they were both panting. Then he slowly let her go. "Good enough?"

She sucked in a breath. "Great start. But can you guarantee there'll be follow-through?"

"I can if you're flexible."

She pretended to misunderstand. "I'm getting more flexible every day." She stretched her arms over her head. "Kickboxing helps."

His gaze heated. "I could come over when I'm on call. But it means I might be able to stay all night and I might have to leave in the middle of flexible sex."

"I'll take that chance."

"Then I'll see you for sure this week." He grinned. "Assuming you're willing to skip a lesson if that happens to be the night I can make it over."

"Depending on my client appointments, maybe I could switch to a midday one." She clasped her hands behind her back and arched her spine. "To stay flexible."

He groaned. "I'm gonna get my shirt and leave before my willpower deserts me." He started down the hall to her bedroom.

Picking up the empty cookie plate and the milk glasses, she took them into the kitchen.

He walked in minutes later fastening the snaps on his shirt. "I'm hoping I'll have Friday night off so we can go dancing at the GG, but if that doesn't work out, I could spend time with you next weekend. Unless you have plans."

"I don't and it would be great if we could go riding. I've managed a couple of trips to the ranch to see Bonnie and Clyde but I haven't ridden either one of them."

"Sounds good to me." He pulled her into his arms and held her gaze. "I love being with you."

"Same here."

A slight crease appeared between his brows and then was gone. He smiled. "Good. I'm going to kiss you once more, and then I'm leaving. It's been a big day and we need—"

"Oh, that's right! You haven't given me a bill for the roof work."

He combed her hair back from her face. "I'm not going to."

"Of course you are. You can email it to me this week."

"Nope. You paid for the materials. The labor is free."

"That's not fair to you. You had three family members over here, too. Everyone should be compensated for all the work."

"Remember the barn raising? Friends and family pitched in without getting paid?"

"But—"

"My family loves you, Olivia, and they want to help you through a tough time with the fire and…well, everything you've been through."

Her throat tightened. "That's very generous. I'll…I'll bake everyone cookies."

"Perfect." Leaning down, he kissed her slowly and tenderly. Then he gave her a tight squeeze and released her. "See you soon. Stay flexible." He left the kitchen.

"Count on it," she called after him. Putting on her glasses, she watched from the kitchen doorway as he scooped up his hat from the couch and settled it on his head.

He glanced back at her, flashed her a grin and touched the brim of his hat in a quick salute. Then he was gone.

Dashing. That was a fitting description for Trevor McGavin. She had a bit of a crush, but what woman wouldn't?

He seemed to have a crush on her, too. How funny if the glasses had something to do with it. She hoped it was only a crush. Just now he'd used the word *love* twice.

Probably meant nothing. People tossed the word around in casual conversation all the time. She was guilty of it herself. Still, that particular word coming from Trevor made her twitchy. She didn't want him to be in love with her. That would ruin everything.

* * *

Coordinating schedules turned out to be more complicated than Olivia had expected. Trevor was on duty at the firehouse Monday, Tuesday and Wednesday night and on call Thursday and Friday.

They made plans for Thursday with the understanding those plans could be torpedoed if they needed him at the station. She juggled her client appointments to make time for a kickboxing class on Thursday morning.

She missed him, but she was busy, too. Fortunately she'd finished filing tax returns for her clients who'd asked for extensions, so her workload was lighter, but she still had a demanding schedule to maintain.

She'd moved her client appointments to Monday morning so that Monday afternoon she and Kendra could shop for plants. That worked for everyone except Ellie Mae Stockton. Olivia ended up scheduling her for noon. She'd grab an energy bar before she met Kendra at one-thirty.

Ellie Mae was a new client. The man who'd been her tax accountant for thirty-two years had retired and moved away, so she'd called Olivia.

She walked in with an old-fashioned briefcase so stuffed with papers it wouldn't close. She plopped the briefcase on the floor and sat in one of two chairs on the far side of it. "Good afternoon, Mrs. Shaw."

"Good afternoon, Mrs. Stockton."

"You can call me Ellie Mae. Everyone does."

"And you can call me Olivia."

"Good. We have that out of the way." Ellie Mae was in her eighties and she obviously took pride in her grooming. She didn't have a single gray hair and her makeup was tastefully applied. Her slacks, blouse and jacket were stylish.

She settled a calm gaze on Olivia. "It was a real shame about your husband. He seemed like a nice fellow."

"He was."

"I admire the way you've carried on since he passed. I've buried two husbands and I know it's not easy."

"No."

Ellie Mae cleared her throat. "Before we get started, I should warn you that I don't think Arnie strictly adhered to the tax code when he prepared my returns."

Olivia blinked. "How so?"

"He gave me a yearly deduction for my vodka purchases. Does that seem right to you?"

"Not really. How did he justify it?"

"He claimed it as a medical expense. He said without my nightly martinis I'd be a total stress case and quite likely would die young. I don't think that would fly with an auditor, do you?"

"No, I'm afraid it wouldn't. Not unless you find a doctor who'll write you a prescription for vodka."

"If I knew such a doctor I'd be his patient in a flash. Thank goodness I've never been audited, then. Since Arnie allowed me that deduction, I always bought the expensive stuff." She leaned back in her chair and gestured to the briefcase. "But I could still be audited for past returns."

"Do you want to file an amended return and eliminate that deduction?"

"Good Lord, no! And pay back taxes when they might never catch up with me? I should say not!"

"Then what would you like to do?"

Ellie Mae lifted the briefcase to her lap. "It's all here. Seven years of deductions for top-shelf vodka. You're a smart lady. If I should get called up by the IRS, I figure you're my best bet for dealing with them."

"Ellie Mae, if the worst happens and you get audited, I doubt I could keep you from paying those taxes. If that's what you're expecting of me, I can't—"

"No, sweetheart, I'm not looking for guarantees. I just need to know I'll have someone in my corner to help me through the process."

"I'm more than willing to be that person. But when it comes to this year's return, you won't be able to deduct your vodka."

"I know. I've already adjusted my budget accordingly."

"Less vodka?"

"Absolutely not. I'll cut back somewhere else. Arnie wasn't following IRS rules and regs, but he was right. Without those martinis, I would've died young."

* * *

Wednesday afternoon the Whine and Cheese Club arrived in their work clothes lugging garden tools. Planting would be followed by what Kendra had called a *cleansing ceremony*. After that they'd celebrate the survival of the house.

Olivia had stocked in food for a buffet dinner and Kendra had assured her the women would bring plenty of wine and their favorite cheeses.

No kidding. Before they started putting plants in the ground, each member of the club brought in two bottles of wine and various packages of cheese. Deidre, wearing denim overalls and a floppy canvas hat to protect her recently colored red hair, stationed herself in the kitchen and organized the selection of whites and reds.

"You want to start with the expensive stuff and save the bargain wine for later when nobody cares." She tucked cheaper whites in the back of the fridge. Then she arranged the good stuff in the front. She managed to find room for all the cheese, too, even though Olivia had filled the shelves with food for dinner.

She watched in admiration. "I'll bet you were good at Tetris as a kid."

"Oh, honey, I was good at all of them. The Whine and Cheese ladies rock those games."

"I can picture that."

"You should have seen us when we crashed Zane's bachelor party last month. We showed those cowboys how it's done."

"They had video games at their bachelor party?" She'd attended Zane and Mandy's wedding but hadn't heard about the bachelor and bachelorette party shenanigans.

"We were all surprised, too, but it turned out to be fun." Deidre shoved the less expensive reds to the back of the counter. "Same principle here. Good stuff first."

"Are you expecting to drink all this?"

"Probably not, but it's never a good idea to run low on wine at a Whine and Cheese event." She glanced at Olivia and laughed. "You look concerned."

"I know you do this all the time, but what about driving home?"

"No worries. That's where Kendra's boys come in. Kendra texts Cody, who hops in the van and collects whichever brothers are available. They get us home safely, along with our vehicles."

"That's awesome."

"Isn't it? It's like those rideshare companies in the big cities, only better 'cause the chauffeurs are so dang cute." She pulled her work gloves out of her overalls pocket. "We'd better get out there. Kendra's hollering at me."

Olivia grabbed her gloves from the laundry room and followed Deidre outside. The other four were gathered around the schematic that Kendra had helped her draw up on Monday showing where each of the plants would go. Most were hardy evergreen types, but she'd bought iris and tulip bulbs for a splash of color in the spring.

Deidre sauntered over to Kendra, who wore jeans and a sweatshirt that had seen better days. She'd pulled her ponytail through the back of an ENHS baseball cap. "What's up, lady? I heard you yelling at me."

Kendra grinned. "Just wanted to make sure you and Olivia weren't in there sampling the vino."

"Would we do that?"

"Before Sunday night at the GG, I would have said no, but after seeing a new side of Olivia, I'm not so sure."

Deidre's eyebrows arched as she looked over at Olivia. "Dancing on the table, were you?"

"*No*." Her cheeks heated. "All I did was sing along with everybody else."

"With gusto!" Kendra said with a wink in her direction. "My no-nonsense accountant, adorable but a wee bit anal, showed up in a bright yellow blouse, a short denim skirt, her contacts in and her hair down."

Judy nodded. "I was there." She smiled at Olivia. "You looked gorgeous."

"Thank you." Her face grew hotter, but despite being embarrassed, she liked the compliment. "It was fun."

"And I missed it." Deidre sighed. "You know how I hate it when I'm not part of the action. Next time I'll find out what's going on at the GG before I leave town."

Kendra pulled gloves out of the back pocket of her jeans. "So where'd you go?"

"Jim took a notion we should see a matinee in Bozeman and stay for dinner."

"Uh-oh," Christine said. "She said Jim's name."

"Wait, wait!" Deidre waved her hands. "I only said Jim because Kendra asked me where—"

"She said it *again*." Jo, Mandy's mom, began to chant. "Jim and Deidre sittin' at the show. What they did you don't wanna know."

Olivia gaped at her. She only knew Jo as a senior officer at the Eagles Nest Bank. Well, and she'd belly danced during the Labor Day Parade.

Deidre rolled her eyes and looked over at Olivia. "Sorry. They get like this."

Christine, a lanky blond, launched into another one. "Jim and Deidre sittin' in a car. Jim yells out *'That's too far!'*"

"Enough!" Deidre held up her hands like a traffic cop. "Drop it. Olivia doesn't need to hear this and we have plants to put in the ground."

Kendra laughed and slung an arm around Deidre's shoulders. "Jim and Deidre sittin' on a chair. Jim says, *Deidre's got a nice—*"

"I mean it!"

"Aw, Deidre, that was a good one." Kendra bumped hips with her. "You have awesome girls. Best boobs of all of us."

"Yeah, okay." Deidre smiled. "I admit it. But we have work to do. Ladies, grab your shovels." She glanced over at Olivia. "You, too. Get a move on, girlfriend. We're burning daylight."

The afternoon and evening were a revelation. Olivia had never known grown women who acted this way. The teasing and jokes continued through the entire planting phase. The comments were goofy, raunchy and hilarious.

They'd all known each other for years, but that didn't explain it. Olivia's mom had known some of her friends for years, too, but they didn't tell each other dirty jokes. At least not when she'd been there. Maybe she needed to ask her mom about that.

Despite the horsing around, the work got done. No one quit until Olivia's shrubs and bulbs were in the ground. When daylight faded, they used the headlights of their vehicles to light the area.

After the dirt was smoothed over the last plant and the mulch was laid down, Kendra lit her sage stick and led them in a march around the house. Then they joined hands in a circle by the walkway to the porch.

"Okay, Jo," Deidre said. "Do your thing."

Jo took a breath and spoke in a clear voice. "Bless this house and all who walk through its doors seeking shelter and solace. Protect it from harm, both without and within. May those who gather here live in peace and joy from this day forward."

The group murmured *Namaste* in unison. Kendra squeezed Olivia's hand and murmured *pass it on.* Olivia squeezed Deidre's hand and the gesture made its way around the small circle.

Gratitude clogged her throat, but then the words tumbled out. "Thank you. Thank you all so much."

"Group hug!" Deidre started it off and soon Olivia was surrounded until Kendra declared it was party time.

Everyone left their shoes and gloves on the porch and jockeyed for a place at the kitchen sink so they could wash up. Olivia got the giggles watching them. She wasn't glad that the forest had burned, never that, but because of it her whole life had changed for the better.

She laid out the buffet dinner on the table where she'd made love to Trevor. The mood of the group must have affected her, because instead of being embarrassed about it, she was amused.

Everyone carried their plates of food and glasses of wine into the living room. She didn't have enough places for everyone to sit, but it didn't matter. Some were happy to take the floor. Clearly they were used to informally hanging out together.

Kendra raised her glass. "To the survival of Olivia's house!"

After everyone drank, Olivia raised her glass. "To the brave firefighters who kept it from burning down!"

Kendra exchanged a quick glance and smile with her before she raised her glass. "Hear, hear!"

Olivia drank and lifted her glass again. "To all of you for being here. I feel incredibly blessed."

"Me, too!" Deidre leaped to her feet. "Olivia, we need music. Got some sort of streaming service?"

"Sure thing." She got up and turned on her compact sound system. "Anything specific?"

A chorus went up from the group. "*Thriller*!"

She found it, and before the first notes left her speakers, the five women had lined up. She stepped to the end of the line even though she'd never danced this in her life.

Slightly panicked, she glanced at Kendra. "What do I do?"

"Follow me."

She did, and it became easier than she could believe. She'd lost her feeling of belonging since Edward had died. But the fire had changed everything. She belonged here.

<u>18</u>

Thursday night seemed eons away, but eventually it arrived. Trevor packed up what he needed to spend the night with Olivia even though he might not get to stay the whole time.

His mom was in the ranch house office entering financial info on the computer when he walked in, a duffel over his shoulder.

She glanced up. "Slumber party?"

"Yeah."

"Have fun."

"Thanks." He started out of the office.

"Hang on. Come back a minute."

"Sure." He turned and lowered himself to one of two chairs she kept in front of her desk. In years past he'd received lectures while sitting here, often with Bryce next to him, in trouble for the same stupid thing.

"I sense you're getting more involved."

"Tough not to. She's great."

"I agree. But do you think she's ready for a new relationship?"

His mom always did cut to the chase. "I don't know. Maybe not."

She regarded him silently for a few seconds. "Telling you what to do would be presumptuous on my part. You're an adult and free to make your own choices."

"You been reading that Parenting 101 book again?"

She made a face. "No, smartass. Talking to your Aunt Jo. She gets credit for those words. I promised her I'd say that to you."

"I'll remember to thank her. It's a good speech."

"As far as it goes."

He laughed. "Okay, say your piece."

"The thing is, I have personal experience with this issue. I've tried to reconstruct where my head was three years after your father died. Clearly I couldn't have conducted a romance. You boys ranged from Cody, who was four, to Ryker, who was eight."

"Olivia isn't in that situation."

"No, and I'm aware that her attitudes are changing. She's growing, opening to new possibilities. But her loyalty to Edward runs deep. Mine to Ian did at that stage, too. Still does."

He nodded. Tough as it was to hear, he needed to keep that in mind.

"We didn't finish our discussion the other night, but the truth is, I pity any man who makes a play for me."

"Why?"

"Because even after twenty-six years, I'll compare him to your dad. He had his share of faults and bad habits like all of us. But I can't remember any of them. All I remember is the good stuff."

"Then I'm in a losing battle?"

"I hope not. I think she'd be a fool to cling to an idealized version of Edward in favor of you, an amazing guy who also happens to be alive."

He grinned. "You sound like Bryce. He said that was my strong point."

"Yeah, I can hear him saying that. But here's the catch. Edward is frozen in time, so he can do no wrong. His halo gets brighter every day that goes by. You're living in the messy present and have a million ways to screw things up."

"Gee, I feel so much better, now. Thanks for the pep talk, Mom."

"You wouldn't want me to shine you on."

"No."

"But like I said, you're an incredible human being and you have a pulse."

"But I have to discount the first part of that sentence because you're my mom. All I truly have going for me is that I have a pulse. That doesn't seem like a dynamic game changer. Any guy walking down the street can claim the same advantage."

"Oh, wait. There's something else. You're very good looking."

"Again, you're my mom. Prejudiced."

"I am, but I've had plenty of others tell me that my five boys are extremely handsome."

"Were they trying to get you to donate to some cause or other?"

"One was, but the rest were saying it unsolicited, with no ulterior motive. I think we can believe them. Handsome and alive. Good advantages to bring to the table." She paused. "But…"

"There's a strong possibility I'm gonna crash and burn."

"I didn't say that."

"But you're thinking it."

"Some of the time. Other times I tell myself to keep my big mouth shut and let whatever happens, happen. It's your life."

He left the chair and went around the desk to give her a kiss on the cheek. "Thanks for caring."

"Always."

He smiled down at her. "I have another thing going for me."

"Yeah?"

"If I crash and burn, I have you and my brothers to help me pick up the pieces."

Her eyes grew moist and she nodded. "That's a biggie."

"Sure is." Giving her shoulder a squeeze, he walked out of the office.

The discussion stayed with him as he drove to Olivia's. On Sunday when he'd said *I love being with you*, she'd responded with *Same here*. Seemed like a deliberate dodge away from the L word.

Had he imagined her flinch when he'd used the word? After talking with his mom, he didn't think so.

He let out a breath. Maybe he was expecting too much, too soon. That would be typical, wouldn't it? Impatience had plagued him all his life.

Funny thing was, he thought she might be falling for him. That special glow in her brown eyes when they made love, the tenderness when she'd touched his cheek the first time he'd been deep inside her, those were the building blocks of something meaningful.

But if she wouldn't admit it to herself, let alone to him, what good was that? Part of the joy in loving someone was being able to say it. A lot.

Instead he'd better watch himself. If he jumped the gun and blurted it out, she might show him the door. Like his mom said, he had so many ways to screw this up.

When he pulled in, she ran out to meet him, her hair loose and flying behind her. She looked like a woman in love. Was she?

Jumping down, he swept her up in his arms and knocked his hat off in his desperation to kiss her. Her mouth was so sweet, so soft and supple. Their separation seemed like weeks, not days. He couldn't get enough.

When he shifted the angle, he nudged her glasses. He started to pull away so she could take them off, but she clutched the back of his head and held him right there, her mouth warm and eager.

Splaying his hands over her cute little ass, he lifted her up and she wrapped her legs around his hips. He started toward the house.

She broke the kiss and took a gulp of air. "Wait."

"Don't want to." His cock strained against his fly.

"Let me show you the plants before it gets dark."

"We'll grab a flashlight later."

"You won't get the full effect."

"I know, but I need—"

"Just take a minute. They did a terrific job."

Not to mention his mom would expect him to comment on the planting effort next time he saw her. He pressed Olivia's hot body closer. "And then we can do this?"

"I promise."

He reluctantly lowered her to the ground and stood back while he sucked in air and tamed his bad boy. "We fogged up your glasses."

"Yep, sure did." She sounded out of breath, too. She pulled off her glasses and polished the lenses with the hem of her knit shirt.

Now that he wasn't kissing her, he paid more attention to the shirt. Swirls of deep pink reminded him of her painting. "Is that a new top?" He hadn't felt a bra under it either. Excellent.

"I bought it today after my kickboxing class. I thought you'd like it since you like the painting."

"You got it so you could wear it for me?"

"I did."

"It looks great." Happiness flooded through him. She must care if she'd do something like that. "I like the pants, too. Soft material."

"It was a set. I decided to deviate from jeans for a change." She put on her glasses. "Where's your hat?"

"I guess it's on the ground next to the truck." He glanced over there. "Right below the door hanging open." That was a first. "Maybe I should fetch my hat and close the door." He headed back.

"Good idea." She sounded amused. "Did you bring a change of clothes?"

"Yes. Yes, I did. Thanks for reminding me." He'd been ready to charge into her house and dive into her bed without his duffel, which contained the all-important package of condoms.

But she'd run out to meet him, which had altered his brain chemistry, temporarily making him stupid. That was his excuse and he was sticking to it.

He dusted off his hat and crammed it on his head. If he didn't get a grip she was liable to figure out he was addle-pated over her. He'd heard an old cowhand say that about a younger guy mooning over his sweetheart. He'd vowed that would never happen to him. He would keep his wits about him.

Yeah, right.

Grabbing his duffel from the passenger seat, he walked back to Olivia. "The plants look good."

"Don't they?" She slipped her hand into his. "I'll give you a tour."

Walking hand-in-hand was something they'd never done before. He liked it.

"So everything's some sort of evergreen shrub except the iris and tulip bulbs. You'll have to wait for spring to see those."

Which indicated she expected him to be around come spring. Another good sign.

"As you can see, we planted four in front of the porch. They're called Little Devil Ninebark."

"Cute."

"We laid down a lot of mulch, too. The empty places are where we put the bulbs, alternating iris and tulips."

"What color?"

"Purple and white for the iris. Yellow and red for the tulips. It'll be pretty. I especially love tulips."

"You know, so do I. I've never thought much about flowers, but tulips are nice."

"Now come around to the side yard. That's where we alternated between some little pines and something called Superstar Spirea."

"You really did plant a lot."

"It helped that there were six of us. Those women are a riot."

He grinned. "Yeah, they are. Whenever the Whine and Cheese ladies show up it's always a good time."

"They worked so hard. You're the first person to see what they accomplished and I wanted to show it off."

"I'm glad you did." He squeezed her hand. "I'll be sure to mention it next time I see Mom."

"Great." She squeezed back. Then she gave him that look, the one that his mom had talked about. Like he was the last piece of fudge on the plate.

"Are we done with the tour, yet?"

"Sure." She drew in a quick breath and her cheeks turned pink. "The other side's just like this and we didn't plant anything in the back. You've seen enough."

"Thank God. Let's go."

"It's quicker if we go in the back door and through the laundry room."

"I'm all for quick." He hustled her around the house, up the back steps and through the back door. Typical laundry room, except for the heavy coil of rope and the miner's hat sitting on the dryer.

He'd ask her about those later. All he cared about now was stripping down, gathering her close and reconnecting with the magic he'd craved since the last time he'd held her.

<u>19</u>

"I'm shameless." Olivia pulled her top over her head and tossed it away. "I bought this outfit so I could skip underwear entirely."

"No panties, either?"

She shrugged. "Why bother?"

"You don't know how happy that makes me." He unsnapped his cuffs.

"I thought you'd like it." She stepped out of her flats and shoved down the drawstring pants. Having an exciting, experienced lover was inspiring. "Done."

"Awesome." He paused to gaze at her. "I love it."

There was that word again. Whenever he said it, a shiver traveled up her spine. "Now that I'm finished, can I help you?"

"There's a package of condoms in the front pocket of my duffel." He pulled open his shirt.

"Got 'em." She put the package on the bedside table. "Let me help you undress."

"I can do it faster." He tossed the shirt across the back of a nearby armchair.

She walked over and took hold of his belt buckle. "Bet I could make it more fun." The person she used to be would *never* have said that.

He blinked, clearly taken aback. Then he gulped. "What do you have in mind?"

"Let me show you." Holding his gaze, she unbuckled his belt and unfastened the metal button on his waistband. Then she drew down the zipper. "Maybe you should sit on the bed."

"Why?"

"So I can pull off your boots."

"Oh." His chest rose and fell rapidly. "Right."

She'd turned the tables on him and he acted slightly confused. There was something endearing about a big manly cowboy who'd given up control. He sat down as she'd asked and she tugged off both boots and his socks.

"Can't say I've ever experienced having a naked woman handle that chore."

She glanced up. "Hope you liked it." She'd never done such a thing in her life. Her inhibitions were dissolving like snowflakes on her palm.

"Oh, I did."

"I think you'll like the next part, too." Kneeling between his thighs, she stroked the cotton briefs stretched across his substantial erection.

He gasped. "Easy."

"I'll be careful." Slowly she peeled down the elastic waistband. Now there was a sight to set a woman on fire.

His voice was tight. "If you do it faster, we can get on with things."

"True. But faster isn't always better." She took off her glasses. "Would you please hold these?"

"Olivia."

"Just for a little while." She put them in his hand so he had no choice but to take them.

"If you're about to do what I think you are, I'm not sure—"

"You mean this?" She swiped her tongue over the tip of his beautiful cock.

He sucked in air.

"Like it?"

"Yes." His jaw clenched. "But I may not...I don't know if I can handle..."

"Want me to stop?" She licked from the base to the top.

He groaned. "Not yet."

"Tell me when." Rising to her knees, she licked, nibbled and finally began to suck. The size of him added to her sense of daring. She was eager to rock his world the way he'd rocked hers.

Judging from his gasps and moans, she was succeeding. His breathing roughened and his big body quivered. Maybe he'd let her take him all the way.

But no. "Olivia." He barely got out her name. "Stop."

She'd promised, so she did. Making him come would have been a trip, but she'd save that experience for another time.

Once she released him, he grasped her by the shoulders and drew her up for a deep, hungry kiss. He pulled back, breathing hard. "Lie on the bed. Please."

"No throwing me down?"

"Not tonight."

As she crawled onto the snowy sheet and stretched out, he shucked his jeans and briefs, tore open the condoms and pulled one from its wrapper.

He cursed softly. "I'm shaking like a leaf."

"Want me to put it on?"

"No. Got it." He climbed in and moved between her thighs. "But don't expect finesse. I'm a wreck."

"I wrecked you?"

"Yeah, and please do it again sometime."

"Gladly."

"Ah, Olivia." He entered her with one firm thrust that lifted her off the mattress. Then he held her gaze. "I'm on the edge. This could be a wild ride."

She wrapped her arms around his sweaty back. "Fine with me."

"Then here goes." Sliding his hands under her ass, he gripped her tight as he began to pump. He started off fast and didn't let up. Sweat beaded his forehead and a damp lock of hair clung there.

The heat in his eyes burned feverishly bright. "Come with me, Olivia."

She came, and kept on coming as he pounded into her. The world spun as his body collided with hers once more and he bellowed her name as the spasms of his climax blended with hers.

The sound of their breathing filled the silence as she lay boneless and panting beneath him. Dinner was in the crockpot, but she might have to stay here until morning. Or sometime next week.

Pushing up on his forearms, he gazed down at her. "Are you okay?"

She smiled. "I'm wrecked."

"In a good way or a bad way?"

"In an extremely good way."

He let out a breath. "That's a relief. That's more intense than I usually...okay, it's never been that intense."

"Really? With all the experience you've—"

"Hey, not *that* much experience." He looked into her eyes. "You pack a punch."

"I do?"

He smiled. "More than you know, apparently."

"It's not me, it's you. You make me want to bring my A game."

He laughed. "You do the same for me, except for just now. I don't know what game I was bringing, but it wasn't at the top of the alphabet. Might have been my Neanderthal game. Primitive forces were at work."

She cupped his face in both hands. "Were you consumed by raw sexuality?"

"That pretty much describes it. Not particularly classy."

"As the other person involved, I have no complaints. Hey, are you hungry? I made dinner."

"Great. I'm starving."

"But no sex on the dining table afterward."

"Yeah, this is better."

"So food, then more sex. Does that work for you?"

"Perfect combination."

"Good." The evening was turning out as great as she'd anticipated. Even better, in fact. Sex had been a given, probably before dinner. Explosive sex had been a bonus.

Earlier she'd set the table and made the salad, so all they had to do was dish up and eat. She served him coffee instead of beer or wine because he was on call. But like Sunday night when they'd sat here eating cookies, she wore only her bathrobe and he'd pulled on his briefs and jeans.

"I served a buffet dinner to the Whine and Cheese Club on this table last night."

He smiled. "And? Were you horribly embarrassed?"

"Nope."

"Glad to hear it." He tucked into his chicken and veggie meal. "This is great."

"Thanks."

"Tomorrow night at the GG is my treat. We're taking a chance, though, going when I'm on call. It's not elegant. We should probably each take our own truck. Not cozy."

"I'd rather do that than not see you at all."

"So would I. But if it turns out to be a screwed-up evening, we can make up for it on the weekend. I want to do some chores for Mom those two days, but other than that, I'm all yours. We'll take Bonnie and Clyde out for sure."

"Sounds lovely."

He picked up his coffee mug. "I'm curious about something, though. Why do you have a big ol' coil of rope and a miner's hat sitting on your dryer?"

Damn it. She'd forgotten he might see that when she took him through the laundry room. Or maybe it was meant to be. He was the person she'd decided to tell. She just hadn't figure on doing it yet.

He put down his coffee. "You're making me nervous, here. I want to believe there's nothing creepy about the rope and miner's hat, but I've seen my share of horror movies and I'm hearing violins screeching in the background."

She sighed. "There's nothing creepy."

"I knew that."

She smiled. "No, you didn't. You were imagining all kinds of weird scenarios."

"All right, I was. So what's with the rope and the miner's hat?"

She took a deep breath. "Okay. Now that Edward's gone, I'm the only person who knows. If I tell you, you have to promise you'll keep it to yourself."

"Or you'll have to kill me?"

"No! It's nothing bad. It's good, very cool, but I don't want anything bad to happen to it."

"You've discovered a dinosaur in the bowels of the earth."

"No, but its old and valuable."

"Gold?"

"I doubt it. If so, we'd have to factor that in." She hesitated. She'd kept the secret for so long.

"Give me your word that you won't tell anyone. Not your mom or your brothers."

"This sounds like a heavy secret. Are you sure you want to trust me with it?"

She considered the question. Once she told him there was no going back. But this was the man who'd helped save her house, who'd led her horses out of the barn with the fire only yards away. This was the man who'd pushed his limits and recruited his family so that she'd have a sturdy new roof on her house before a storm hit.

But more than that, this was the ethical man who'd responded to her repressed wild impulses yet had always respected her boundaries. If she couldn't trust Trevor McGavin with this secret, she couldn't trust anyone.

She took a deep breath. "It's a cave."

"A cave like bears live in?"

"No. An undiscovered cave with stalactites and stalagmites. Still dripping, still growing. Edward and I explored enough of it to be reasonably sure no human has been in there except us."

"Wow."

"It's huge. Beautiful. A natural treasure. But if the wrong people get ahold of it and try to monetize it, that would be tragic."

"Do you have a plan?"

"A loose one based on another cave in Arizona where they managed to keep it pristine. But I'd rather not tackle the project alone. Will you help me?"

His expression softened. "Of course."

"Great. That's so great." A weight lifted off her shoulders.

"There's only one tiny problem."

"What's that?"

"I'm claustrophobic."

20

A cave. Trevor wanted to bang his head against the wall. It figured that his best chance to be Olivia's hero would involve going into a cave. Not just any cave, either. An undeveloped one filled with darkness and tight spaces.

He took a shaky breath. "Are there bats?"

"Yes. A whole colony of them. Are you afraid of bats?"

"Not bats themselves, but bats in an enclosed space aren't my favorite thing." Edward had probably loved going into this cave and dodging bats.

"You don't have to go down there."

"I think I do. If I'm going to help you advocate for it, I should know what I'm talking about."

"Do you know why you have claustrophobia?"

"Sure. Got stuck in an old mine shaft on ranch property when I was four years old. We were all out exploring, playing frontier like we used to do, and we found this shaft. I wandered in, fell down a side tunnel and couldn't climb out."

"You must have been so scared."

"Terrified. Ryker and Zane tried to get me out because they knew Mom would be furious. They were supposed to watch out for Bryce and me. But they couldn't get me out, which meant I was down there a long-ass time while they tried all sorts of things that ultimately failed."

"Then they went after your mom."

"Yep, and she got the sheriff's department. I was rescued after about three hours. I was hysterical by then." He shuddered. "Still gives me the willies. Mom had forgotten the mine was even there. She had it boarded up and fenced off. I still avoid it."

"You really don't have to go into the cave. I just need someone to help me figure out the steps I should take to assure it'll be in good hands."

"I'll do that, too, but I'm going down there. How does Saturday sound?"

She shook her head. "Don't put yourself through it."

"I'm thinking about one o'clock would be good. Then afterward we can drive to the ranch and take Bonnie and Clyde out. We can strategize during the ride, when no one else is around."

"Trevor, no. I have some pictures on my phone. I can show you those. I can even take more to give you an idea of what it's like. That's enough for you to—"

"I'm going down there, Olivia. If you can conquer your fear of heights, I can conquer this. It's important and I—" His phone buzzed and he pulled it out of his pocket. "Damn."

"The station?"

"Yeah." He was in motion instantly, heading for the bedroom for his shirt and boots. He came back carrying his boots and duffel. His shirt hung open.

"You're taking your duffel?"

"I'd better." He sat on a dining room chair to pull on his socks and boots. "No telling how long this will take. Kitchen fire. If it hasn't spread, I could be done in a few hours, but I should bunk at the station."

"How about leaving your duffel and coming back here?"

"Like I said, it could be anytime. Maybe even three or four in the morning. That's not fair to you."

Pushing away from the table, she walked into the kitchen and returned with a key. "Take this." She laid it next to him. "At the very least, shower and change for work here. Then I'll know you're back safe."

He glanced up in time to see the worry that flashed in her eyes. "I'll do that. But I'll be fine. I'm a safety-first kind of guy, remember?"

"You said it yourself. Fire is unpredictable."

"Yes, but I'm working with a great crew." Pocketing the key, he wrapped his arm around her waist and pulled her in for a quick kiss. "Don't wait up."

"I won't." Her smile was temptation personified. "But wake me when you get back."

"I will." Leaving was tough, but his spirits were high. She was into him. She'd trusted him with an important secret. She'd given him a key to her house because she needed to know he was safe after fighting the fire. All good signs that they were bonding.

The kitchen fire was nasty but they had it out in a couple of hours. Then a second call came in. Fire in an old shed. Owners were out of town. Neighbors were upset.

Trevor was on the hose directing the spray when the shed exploded.

"Everybody down!" Ortega yelled orders as flaming debris sailed through the air.

Something heavy landed on Trevor's shoulder, pinning him to the ground along with the hose. He struggled, but he wasn't going anywhere. Then the back end of the hose caught fire. He watched the fire creep closer to his turnout. Shit.

His mom would be furious if he ended up burned or dead. She believed in what he was doing, but that didn't mean she'd be okay if he died. She'd cry a lot, too.

Ryker would understand, but the rest of his brothers would be pissed that he'd made their mother cry, even if it was for a good cause. They'd sit around chewing him out for getting himself killed. He wasn't so enamored of that happening, either. After all, he'd just found Olivia…

Olivia…dear God, Olivia didn't deserve another tragedy in her life. He tried to move whatever it was, must be a part of a roof beam, but he stayed put, cheek resting on the bare ground.

"Man down! Man down!" The ground shook as boots pounded the earth. "Hose! Spray the damn hose!"

Swap. A blast of water hit the burning hose...and him. Sputtering, he lifted his head as far as he could from the ground. Didn't matter. He squeezed his eyes shut and held his breath as mud splattered his face.

The spray stopped, which must mean the hose fire was out. But his face was coated with mud. His eyes burned and his mouth tasted like garbage.

"Okay, let's get him out of there. On three. One, two, *three*." The beam lifted.

He pushed upward and his arms held his weight. Maybe nothing was broken.

"Take it easy, Trev." The chief put a restraining hand on his shoulder. "Don't try to go anywhere yet, okay?"

Spitting out the mud, he stayed where he was while the EMTs did their thing and Ortega rejoined the crew. Other than some tenderness in his shoulder, he checked out okay. The EMTs helped him to his feet and handed him a towel for his face.

"Thanks." Taking off his gloves, he wiped most of the grime off and gave it back. Then he looked over toward the shed just as it collapsed in a shower of sparks. Under Ortega's watchful eye, the crew kept giving it water until the flames finally sputtered out.

The crew started mopping up and the chief headed back toward Trevor. "You doing okay, McGavin?"

"I'm fine. Just filthy."

"Maybe you should take a ride to Eagles Nest General and get a few x-rays."

Trevor shook his head. "Don't need to. I'll have some bruises, but nothing worse than that." An emergency room visit would cause a delay. As soon as he was done here, he had places to go and a certain woman to see.

"Well, pay attention for the next few days in case something crops up."

"I will."

Ortega turned to gaze at the smoking rubble. "All things considered, we got off easy, especially if you don't experience any aftereffects."

"Why did it explode like that?"

"Ammunition." Ortega sighed. "Shells are everywhere. Near as I can figure, he'd rigged up some homemade alarm system that shorted out."

Trevor looked over at the chief. "Do you ever get discouraged?"

"About what?"

"Human stupidity."

"Nah. I've done some stupid things in my day. Just my good luck I didn't make a mess like this."

"What a great attitude."

He grinned. "That's why they pay me the big bucks. Listen, you've turned into a hell of a firefighter. If you ever want to go full-time and draw a paycheck, I can find room in the budget."

Trevor met his gaze. "I'm honored that you'd make the offer. It means a lot."

"You'll consider it?"

"No, 'fraid not. I wouldn't want to give up the construction work. I get a charge out of building things."

"Yeah, I understand. Me, too."

"Yeah? What do you build?"

"Doll houses with my daughter."

"No kidding?"

Ortega laughed. "Not a manly image, is it?"

"It's not that, it's just—"

"Not what you'd expect from a six-five, two-twenty firefighter." He held up his gloved hands. "It's a challenge to work with something that delicate."

"I doubt I could. Not now. Made some models when I was a kid with smaller hands, but—"

"I didn't think I could, either, but she asked me and I wasn't about to say no. It brings us together."

"Nice."

"It is nice. Since her mom and I split, I needed a way to connect with her. At first I did most of it, but now she does the lion's share and I help."

"I wouldn't mind seeing one sometime."

"I have pictures." He took off one glove so he could scroll through the photos on his cell. "Here's the last one we finished." He handed over the phone. "We're giving it to a girl at her school who doesn't have much to play with."

Trevor enlarged the picture to examine the detail on the green and white Victorian. "That's amazing. What a cool project." He handed back the phone.

"We like it." The chief turned to survey the area again. "Well, looks like we can wrap this one up." He glanced at his phone. "Night's almost gone. Gonna bunk at the station?"

"Nope. Once I shower off the mud, I'll be heading...home." It wasn't true, but in a way, it was. He was at home in Olivia's arms.

A half-hour later, he let himself in as quietly as possible. After relocking the door, he took off his boots before walking back to the bedroom. He wanted her, especially after the night he'd had. His body hummed with tension, but he wouldn't—

"I'm awake." Her sleepy voice came from the shadows covering the bed.

"You can go back to sleep." He stripped off his clothes. "I'll just climb in and go straight to sleep, myself."

Her laugh was low and seductive. "Fat chance."

"I mean it." He slipped under the covers. "It's late. Or early, whichever way you want to look at it."

"I don't care." Wrapping her warm arms around his neck, she aligned her soft body with his. "But you might. We can sleep if you want. You're probably tired."

He pulled her in tight. "Does it feel like I'm tired?"

"Not particularly." She wiggled closer. "You smell like smoke."

"Probably do." He rolled her to her back and settled in, keeping his weight on his forearms. "At least I'm not muddy."

"You were gone a while. Must have been a tough fire."

"First one wasn't so bad. The second one was challenging. But I don't want to talk about fires." He covered her mouth with his and groaned with pleasure. So good.

She heated up fast, sliding her hands free and cupping his ass.

He lifted a fraction away from the kiss. "Trying to tell me something?"

"Uh-huh." She pressed her fingers into his glutes.

"What?"

Her two-word response was earthy and to the point.

"How you talk." He reached for the package on the bedside table.

"Wanted to be clear."

"Message received." He eased back so he could put on the condom. Then he reclaimed his position between her thighs and pushed deep. "Is this what you had in mind?"

She sighed. "Oh, yeah."

"How about this?" He began stroking, slow and steady.

"That works." She rose to meet him. "Missed you."

"Missed you, too."

"Glad you're safe."

"So am I." Five minutes ago his shoulder had ached something fierce, but not anymore. Breathing in the sweet, womanly scent of her, he kept the rhythm steady as he leaned down to drop a light kiss on her parted lips. "I could do this forever."

"What about food?"

"Who cares?"

"And sleep?"

"Don't need it." He picked up the pace. "Just need...this." *And you. I need you.*

Her breathing quickened. "Me, too." Her first spasm squeezed his cock. "Come with me."

"Love to." He bore down.

She gasped out his name.

"I'm here. I'm here, Olivia." When she erupted with a wild cry, he drove home, shuddering in the grip of a powerful release. Closing his eyes, he gave thanks for this moment. It wasn't everything he wanted, not yet, but he was getting closer.

<u>21</u>

Trevor called late in the day on Friday. A firefighter had come down sick and the chief had asked him to finish out the shift. That knocked out their plans for dinner at the GG plus the cave visit and horseback riding on Saturday.

He'd be available on Sunday, though. Once again, Olivia tried to talk him out of going into the cave but he was adamant.

On Sunday afternoon, she walked out to meet him. Running like she had on Thursday didn't seem right. Even the weather contributed to the somber mood. Grey clouds covered the top of the mountains and a few drifted overhead, intermittently blocking the sun. A cool breeze made her shiver.

He climbed from the cab with a jaunty smile, but she wasn't fooled. He was wound tight. He shoved back his hat and kissed her with intensity, as always, but underneath the hot passion, she sensed a river of fear.

He ended the kiss and sighed. "Sorry about Friday night and Saturday."

"No worries." She cupped his face in her hands. "It gave me a chance to think about this adventure and I've put several battery-operated lanterns down there. That might help."

"Great idea. Thank you."

"The rope's already in place. I brought the miner's hats out to the porch. Figured you'd want to get on with this."

"You bought me a hat? I thought of it but I didn't have time."

"It's Edward's."

"Oh. Right." He didn't look happy about that.

"I'll go get them."

"Sure. Okay. I'll wait here."

She paused. "Trevor, you really don't have to go down—"

"Yes, I do. I appreciate the loan of the hat."

She hurried back to the porch. She'd almost bought a new hat for Trevor when she'd picked up the lanterns. Then she'd dismissed the idea as being overly protective of his feelings. Now she wished she'd done it.

When she returned, he was staring at the clouds.

She looked up at the sky. "Do you think it'll rain? Because if you do, then we'd be better off not going now." His distress tore at her. She'd ditch the plan in a heartbeat.

He grimaced. "It won't rain. Not for a couple of hours, anyway." He took off his Stetson and laid it in the truck. "Let's go."

"Here's your...the hat."

His flinch was barely perceptible. He tucked the hat under his arm. "Thanks. Lead the way."

She started down the grassy hillside that sloped away from the house. "I always take a different route so I don't wear a path."

"I see paths, though." His breathing was slightly uneven.

"Critters made those. None of them lead to the cave."

"How big is the hole?"

"Small, but you'll fit. It's overgrown with grass so you have to search for the metal stake we drove in the ground. We never rode Bonnie and Clyde in this direction once we found it."

"What about the fire?"

"Doesn't seem to have affected the cave, thank goodness. Maybe because it's so deep."

"How deep?"

Damn. She shouldn't have mentioned depth. Now that she had, she couldn't pretend she didn't know. "It's a twenty-five-foot rope. There's a gradual slope to the bottom."

He sucked in a breath. "Okay."

"You don't—"

"Olivia." The quiet warning in his voice indicated the subject was closed.

"All right." She circled around the area and came at it from the backside. "This is it. See the stake?" She pointed it out.

"I do, but you sure camouflaged it well."

"Thanks. It was a priority." She gave him what she hoped was an encouraging smile. "I'll go first." She put on her hat and turned on the light. "Have you ever done rope climbing?"

"Yep. Both in high school and firefighter training."

"Edward and I had to teach ourselves. Neither of us had ever done it. We had to build up our strength so we could make it to the bottom and back up."

He gave her a wry smile. "But now you're a mighty kickboxer."

"That definitely helps." She took a deep breath. "I'll call up to you when I'm at the bottom. I'll talk you down."

"Right." He put on the miner's hat and shoved his hands in his pockets.

"I wish I had somebody else here, someone to coach you at the start, like when you asked Bryce to come by when I was on the ladder."

He shook his head. "Until we have a plan, we don't want anyone else knowing about this."

"No, we don't." She hated leaving him, but there was no help for it. "Remember, there's light at the bottom. It's not a big dark hole."

"And you'll be there."

"Yes." Her stomach did a flip-flop. He was counting on her to get him through this. That was some serious trust. "See you in a few minutes." Grasping the rope, she lay on her stomach and eased through the opening. "This is how I do it. You may have a different idea."

"Nope."

She gazed up at him. His face was an emotionless mask that likely hid his terror. But recent experience had taught her that simply doing the thing could eliminate the fear. The first step was the hardest, though.

Shimmying down in record time, she looked up at the small bit of daylight above her. "Trevor McGavin, come on down!"

His short bark of laughter was followed by the daylight being blocked when he wedged his big body into the opening. "It's too damn small!"

"No, it's not. Push yourself past that point."

He did, dislodging small stones and loose dirt that tumbled around her. The opening was a little bigger now. That was okay. Eventually, when enough protections were in place, the opening could be enlarged.

As he started down the rope, he began cussing. Continuously. She'd planned to talk him through it, but he wouldn't have heard her and she was too busy covering her mouth to hold back laughter. He used words she'd never heard before in an unending stream of filthy language.

His descent was even faster than hers. In no time, he stood before her, white and shaking. His shirt was soaked.

"You did it."

"Yeah." Gulping for air, he glanced at the lanterns on the cave floor. "Thanks for the lights."

"There's more in the next room." She dropped to her hands and knees. "We just have to go through here."

"Shit. I thought I was done with crawling through holes."

"There's more to see in the next room. Come on. You're this far. You might as well keep going."

"Guess so, especially if you're going."

She maneuvered through the opening and stood on the other side waiting for him.

He had to work to get his shoulders past the narrow space, but eventually he made it and got to his feet.

"There are more, bigger chambers, but this is my favorite."

He nodded, but he remained focused on her.

She'd have to calm him down if she expected him to appreciate where he was. She gestured to the flat rock. "Have a seat. Catch your breath."

"Okay." He sat down, closed his eyes and swallowed. "That was rough."

"I could tell. I've never heard anyone swear that much." Sitting beside him, she took his big hand and laced her fingers through it. His skin was clammy.

Opening his eyes, he focused on her, but nothing else. He cleared his throat. "Bryce and I used to have cussing contests. The person who could go the longest without repeating anything won whatever we'd bet on that day."

"It's a unique skill."

"I honestly didn't know I'd do that. I apologize if I offended you."

"I thought it was funny. But I didn't want to laugh when you were going through hell." She squeezed his hand. "Trevor, look around," she said gently. "There's beauty here if you can allow yourself to see it."

"I'm afraid if I look around I'll remember that we're under tons of dirt with only one way out."

"We're safe. This cave has been here for thousands of years. It's not like some rickety mine shaft built by humans. The bats must think it's safe if they've chosen it for raising their babies."

"Yeah, I can hear them. Will they fly in here?"

"Probably not. We're talking and shining lights around. They wouldn't want to move toward something that might be dangerous to them." She squeezed his hand again. "Take a look at the formations. They're amazing."

"And that's why I'm here, so I can help you advocate for their preservation."

"Exactly."

Drawing in another deep breath, he slowly turned his head. Then he blinked. "Oh, wow."

"Told you."

Lifting his head, he surveyed the ceiling about twelve feet above them. "What's that sound?"

"Water and minerals dripping off the end of those stalactites. The drips land on the stalagmites below and gradually build it up while the stalactites are growing, too."

"We studied that in school. Eventually they meet."

"After a really long time. Then they look like that one over there." She pointed to an amber colored formation where she'd placed one of the lanterns.

"So if this happens in lots of caves, what's special about this one?"

"It's no longer happening in most of the caves where humans have come in and taken over. If they don't know any better, they end up disturbing the delicate balance that allows the cave to keep growing. The dripping stops and the cave…well, it dies."

"Hm." He slowly took in his surroundings again. "That would be a damned shame."

She let out a breath. He got it. "But the cave needs to be seen and appreciated. It would be a fabulous educational opportunity."

He nodded. "And good for Eagles Nest."

"It would be. But I don't have the resources to develop it or protect it. I need the state to handle that."

"Makes sense."

"I've only been here six years, though. I haven't paid much attention to state politics. You've lived here all your life."

"Yeah, but that doesn't mean I know anything about state government. At election time, I figure out who to vote for. That's about it."

"Then we can research it together."

"Or we can talk to someone who already has a connection there. But it means letting someone else in on the secret."

"Who's that?"

"Zane."

"Oh! I didn't think of that. Of course he'd have to get permits and licenses and stuff for his raptor program."

"Would you trust him with this?"

"Yes, but...one more person could easily become two."

"You mean if he told Mandy."

"Right, and after all, they're married, so I hate to ask him to keep a secret from her. And she's trustworthy, but then she might feel it was safe to tell just her mom. And her mom might mention it to Kendra, thinking Kendra must already know. That's how word gets out, one person at a time."

"Especially in a town the size of Eagles Nest." He gazed at her. "Okay, here's how I see it. The sooner you get the state to take over, the more likely the cave will be protected before word gets out."

"I agree."

"Zane is the quickest path to that goal because he already has contacts. Now that he's running a larger facility, he deals with the folks in Helena all the time. We need him. But he can't tell Mandy."

"Is it fair to ask that of him?"

"Maybe not, but we have no choice. He knows how things are around here regarding gossip. He'll want to help you push this through ASAP so he doesn't have to keep it from Mandy for too long."

"You're making a lot of sense. All right. I like that plan."

"Good." He glanced around. "I get why this is so important. I won't pretend that I'm thrilled about caves, but when you come upon something that no one else has ever seen..."

"It's mind-boggling. I mean, how often does that happen?"

"For most people? Never. And I'm only the third person to see it." His color had improved. His shoulders had relaxed a bit, too.

"As far as I know, we're the only three. Edward and I didn't explore every chamber, but wherever we went, we found no other footprints, no primitive tools, no signs of a cooking fire. Just us and the bats."

"How many bats are there?"

"I have no idea and you don't want to know."

"You're right. I don't. But I can already tell I'll get better at this. Next time I promise not to swear."

"You'd come down again?"

He regarded her steadily. "This cave is important to you."

"Very important."

"Then it's important to me, too."

"Thank you." She was grateful for the support, support she desperately needed.

She wished he was doing it for the sake of the cave, though. That might be a part of his motivation because he seemed impressed with this discovery. But his last statement left no doubt. Mostly he was doing it for her.

22

Trevor made it out of the cave more gracefully than he'd gone in. Olivia waited until he was above ground before she turned off the lanterns, which he appreciated.

In retrospect, he was embarrassed about the way he'd cussed during his descent. No telling what he'd said, either. The words had spilled out of him in an involuntary rush. She hadn't seemed to mind, but he hadn't come off as heroic as he would have liked.

Still, he'd survived the experience without passing out. He'd been super worried he might do that. If he'd lost consciousness while hanging onto that rope, he could have broken his neck or hurt Olivia by landing on top of her.

Dreaming up imaginative swear words had kept him from thinking about descending twenty-five feet beneath the surface of the earth. The mine shaft had only been about ten. He doubted he'd ever be a fan of underground exploration, but those formations had captured his imagination. He was glad he'd gone down there and he'd do it again, as many times as she needed him to.

She was stoked about the way the cave adventure had gone and he was happy about that, too. Watching Olivia get excited about an idea was a major high for him. That she'd included him in the planning stages of this project gave him hope for the future.

He took off Edward's miner's hat the minute he was out of the cave, though. He'd buy another one before he went down there again.

But he was eager to deliver on his end of the bargain and hook her up with the right people at the state level. Zane would have info but he could be on a Wild Creek Ranch trail ride right now.

As they neared the house, he pulled his phone from his pocket. "Mind if I call Mandy and find out where Zane is this afternoon? He could be on a trail ride with Mom and not available. But if we're going to the ranch for a ride, maybe he'd be able to meet us for a private chat about this."

"Good idea."

"We'll only talk to Zane and we can keep the details vague if you want."

"No, I don't want that. When we meet him, I want to tell him the whole story. If he's going to help get me to the right state agency, he should know what it's for. I might not tell the state official the details until I'm sure they're on the same page with me, but I can tell Zane."

"Then I'll call Mandy." He sat on Olivia's porch steps and located the number.

Mandy answered, but she seemed distracted instead of her usual peppy self.

"Hope I didn't catch you at a bad time. I wondered where Zane is this afternoon. I'd like to talk with him about something."

"He's...um...right here, Trev."

After what sounded suspiciously like a rustle of sheets, Zane came on the line. "Hey, bro. What's up?"

Trevor groaned. "I interrupted something, didn't I?"

"Yeah, but it's okay. I marked my place."

In the background, Mandy chuckled.

"Damn, I'm sorry. Tell Mandy I'm sorry, too."

"I will. Whatcha need?"

"Advice. About something important. Olivia and I are coming over to the ranch to ride Bonnie and Clyde for an hour or so and I thought maybe—"

"I'll be there when you get back. See you then."

"Thanks."

"Welcome." Zane disconnected.

Olivia sat beside him on the steps. "What was that all about?"

"I called while they were having sex."

"In the middle of the afternoon?"

"What's wrong with that?"

She flushed. "Nothing. I was only saying...oh, forget it! I don't know what I was saying."

He smiled. "I think you were trying to say that a little afternoon sex would be great right now."

"Aren't we supposed to go riding?"

"We can do both."

They did, too, enjoying a quickie in her bedroom followed by a short but energetic ride that gave Bonnie and Clyde a decent workout. Trevor took Edward's chestnut gelding, Bonnie. That meant using Edward's saddle because it had been built specifically for that horse. He chose not to think about it.

No one was around as they unsaddled the horses so he figured he could ask the questions that had popped into his head during the ride. "If you'll be deeding your land over to the state at some point, are you planning to rebuild the barn now?"

"I'm debating." She grabbed a brush from the grooming tote and swept it over Clyde's broad back. "I miss these guys, but they seem to love it over here and I can come see them and ride whenever I want. If the project goes the way I hope and the state acquires the land, there will be no reason to have a barn there."

"What about the house?"

"That's a different story. I want it used for something, either an information center, offices, caretaker's quarters...something. I'd hate to see it bulldozed and with the new roof and landscaping I can't see why they would. It's a ready-made asset."

"It is." But she wouldn't be living there anymore, as he'd expected. That took some getting used to.

"I'm so grateful to you for the roof and the Whine and Cheese ladies for planting the shrubs." She held up the brush. "Need this?"

"Sure." He came around and got it. "What about you? Have you figured out where you'll live?"

"Not specifically. After living there, I'm used to a more rural setting. I doubt I'd choose to live in town."

"But which town?" His chest tightened.

"Eagles Nest, of course." She gazed at him. "Did you think I'd leave?"

He shrugged. "Maybe. I mean, you could."

"No, I couldn't. This is my home. Not just that house, but the beautiful mountains, the friendly town, my great clients, my thoughtful friends. So many reasons to stay."

Including me? He wouldn't ask. "Good. I'm glad."

Zane showed up at the end of the grooming session and walked with them over to the pasture gate. He opened it and they turned Bonnie and Clyde out to graze.

"They seem to have acclimated." Zane watched them trot over to join the horses who had stayed home from the day's trail ride.

"They sure have." Olivia leaned her forearms on the gate. "I've told Kendra she's welcome to try them on a trail ride, although she probably needs to take both and not just one."

"She mentioned that to me. We might give it a shot next weekend."

Trevor glanced over at Zane. "Who's out there today?"

"Cody and Faith. Mom and Aunt Jo are shopping in Bozeman and Jim's at home repairing some of our tack."

"So that's why it seems so quiet."

"Yeah." Zane nudged back his hat. "It's not often nobody's around. What did you two need advice about?"

Trevor looked over at Olivia. "Since no one's here, how about we go up to the house and grab something cool to drink while you fill Zane in?"

"Sounds good. I'll get my phone from the truck."

"What do you need your phone for?"

"Pictures."

"Oh. Right." Just his luck Edward would be in them. He didn't remember what the guy looked like. He wouldn't mind keeping it that way.

Moments later they'd settled into the living room, Trevor and Olivia on the couch and Zane in an easy chair, each with a chilled bottle of beer.

Olivia focused on Zane. "Before I start this story, I have a huge request."

"All right."

"What I'm about to tell you can't go anywhere. I'll specifically ask you not to tell Mandy."

He frowned. "I don't keep secrets from her. I mean, birthdays and Christmas, sure, but not major things."

Trevor leaned forward. "Well, bro, this is a major thing and you can't tell her."

"Will it affect her in any way?"

"Not negatively," Olivia said. "It could turn out to be a positive, though."

"And I have to promise this before you tell me anything?"

She nodded. "Trevor and I talked this through when we considered bringing you in on the project. It's highly sensitive. I trust Mandy. I trust the whole extended family. But the more people who know about this, the more likely we'll have a leak. We can't afford one."

Zane stared at her. "Has an alien ship crash-landed on your property?"

"No, nothing like that."

"Then you must have discovered gold or maybe oil."

"Don't try to guess it," Trevor said. "You won't. We just need your word that you won't tell Mandy."

"Damn." Zane scrubbed a hand over his face. "Now I *really* want to know, but I hate that I have to keep it from her."

"You'll be able to tell her eventually," Olivia said.

"How soon?"

"I don't know yet."

"Perfect." He flopped back in his chair. "A secret I might have to keep from Mandy for years."

"Maybe not," Olivia said. "It depends on…well, a lot of things. Are you in?"

"Of course I'm in." He took a deep breath. "Nobody could resist a buildup like that. But if I get in trouble with Mandy over this, I expect you two to help smooth things over."

"We will." Olivia glanced at Trevor and he nodded.

"Then lay it on me."

She cleared her throat. "Four years ago, Edward and I were wandering the property and found a hole. Air was coming out of it. We did some research, figured out it was a cave, got rope and explored it."

Zane sat forward. "There's a cave on your property? That's cool but I don't see why—"

"Not just an ordinary cave. It has at least five chambers, maybe more. Some are ceiling height, others cathedral height. We found no evidence anyone had ever been there."

"That's impressive."

"And it's still forming, still alive. You can hear the stalactites dripping."

"Really?"

Trevor nodded. "You can. Pretty amazing."

Zane's gaze snapped to his. "How do you know this?"

"I was there this afternoon."

"With your ear to the hole?"

"No, I went down."

Zane stared at him. "Into the cave."

"Yes. Saw the first room. Saw and heard the dripping. And the bats."

"That's...hard to believe." His attention swung to Olivia. "Are you aware that Trev's extremely claustrophobic?"

"He told me. I tried to talk him out of going but he insisted."

"Hm." Zane exchanged a glance with Trevor that clearly said *what the hell*?

He shrugged. "I had to." He wasn't about to explain that he loved this woman and would walk through fire for her. Or descend into a big black hole. "Olivia put lanterns down there. That helped."

"I see."

Olivia pulled out her phone. "I didn't take pictures today, but I've taken a bunch other times." She scooted closer to Trevor. "It might make this easier if you come over here next to me so I can show both of you."

Trevor scrambled for an excuse to bow out. Couldn't find one, so he moved over to make room for all three of them with Olivia in the middle.

Then the torture began. She narrated the pictures with such enthusiasm that he had to look or appear rude. He glanced at selfies of her with Edward, a glasses-wearing, smiley guy wearing the miner's hat. He was probably nice. Probably a considerate husband. A good lover.

Stop it! He guzzled some beer. More pictures. Some were just the formations but most included Edward, relaxed and happy, not even slightly claustrophobic. The love in Olivia's voice twisted the knife deeper.

She seemed totally caught up in her memories and her dreams for this project. He doubted she remembered he was sitting there. He wished to hell he wasn't. The picture show seemed endless but maybe lasted five minutes. At the end of it, his bottle was almost empty.

"That's incredible," Zane said. "And nobody knows?"

"Just the people sitting on this couch." Olivia tucked her phone away. "But it's too valuable to keep secret. I want the state to take it over, but their stewardship needs to be mindful or the cave will be ruined. Trevor said you knew the people in Helena I should talk to."

"I do. In fact, I was going up there on Wednesday. If you can clear your schedule for the day, you're welcome to ride along. I can introduce you and you can decide how much you want to reveal."

"Not much at first. Not until I'm convinced they'll do this right."

"I have confidence in the woman I'll introduce you to. Preservation of natural resources is her top priority."

She let out a breath. "Just what I've hoped for. Maybe the Edward Shaw Caverns will become a reality, after all."

Trevor choked on his last swallow of beer. *The Edward Shaw Caverns?* She'd failed to mention that she was naming the cave after her dead husband.

He should have seen it coming. But he hadn't and now he was the poor lovelorn sap who'd agreed to help her turn this cave into a memorial for the only man she'd ever loved or ever would love. Perfect.

23

Trevor was silent on the drive back. When Olivia attempted conversation, he responded with a word or two but didn't hold up his end. That wasn't like him, or at least not like the person she'd known the past few weeks. He'd never been moody before.

He pulled up in front of the porch instead of parking. He left the engine running.

She turned to him. "Aren't you coming in?"

He met her gaze, his expression bleak. "I have some thinking to do. That's better done alone."

"I should have warned you about the pictures."

"I knew you had them. You offered to show them to me so I wouldn't have to go down into the cave. I had a fair idea of what to expect."

"But they bothered you. I was hoping they wouldn't, just like I hoped wearing his hat wouldn't bother you."

"Or riding his horse and using his saddle."

"Yes!" She unbuckled and turned more fully toward him. "You seemed fine with that."

"I forced myself not to think about it so we could enjoy our ride."

"Oh."

"Look, I know it's stupid and juvenile to be jealous of a dead man. I thought I could be your lover without expecting anything but friendship in return. But I can't. What we have here is a love triangle."

"How can we when Edward's gone?"

"Simple. I love you, but you love him. There's your triangle."

She gulped. "You…you love me?"

"I'm surprised you don't know. Zane knows."

"How could he?"

"Love is the only thing that got me down that rope. Well, and swearing. But mostly love."

Her heart thumped painfully. "Oh, dear."

"I worked through some of my thoughts on the way over here. I'll continue to help wherever I can with the cave. But I can't…" He choked and cleared his throat. "I can't make love to you anymore." He said it fast and sucked in a quick breath.

"Oh." She gripped the front of her shirt because she had to hold onto something and that was the only thing handy. She hadn't brought a purse and she wasn't going to touch him. They both might break if she did.

"See, I was telling myself that if I stuck it out, I had a chance. You might say you'd never love anyone but Edward, but I was hoping you'd gradually change your mind. You'd start to love me. Not that you'd stop loving him, but you'd find a place in your heart for me, too."

Her throat hurt. It hurt bad. "I'm so sorry." Her voice was only a whisper.

"I know you are. I can see it in your eyes. I don't want to make you cry, Olivia. That's the last thing I want to do." He cleared his throat again. "But I'm gonna have to ask you to get out and go in the house, now."

She nodded. Fumbling with the door, she got herself out, closed the door and hurried up the steps. He pulled away after she made it inside. He was such a gentleman. Even when he was suffering he was considerate.

She wandered through the house with one hand pressed to her tight chest and the other to her churning stomach. When she closed her eyes, she saw his expression before she'd turned away. Hopeless.

She cried out and the sound echoed in the quiet house. How could she hurt him like that? He was such a good man! What an idiot she'd been to think that he could handle being friends and lovers but nothing more. Or that she could handle it.

Where was the fun, the lighthearted, sexy romping in the sheets? How had it turned into agonizing pain? What a mess. What a stupid, horrible mess.

But there was the cave. Thanks to Trevor and now Zane, she was on her way to making the project a reality. That was bigger than love triangles and broken hearts, right?

Future generations would benefit from the natural wonders of Edward Shaw Caverns. Edward would be remembered, as he should be, for discovering them.

She sank down to the couch. "I love you, Edward. I love you so much." She squeezed her eyes shut and concentrated on envisioning Edward's face. It wouldn't come up for her.

But Trevor's did.

* * *

On Wednesday, Olivia and Zane spent most of the two-hour drive to Helena talking about the cave. But when they reached the outskirts of the city, she gathered her courage and asked how Trevor was doing.

"He's a little rough around the edges, but he'll pull through. It's not like this has never happened to him."

Pain sliced through her. "Other women have hurt him?"

"He's twenty-six. By that time most guys have had their hearts broken at least once and often more than that."

"That's terrible."

"That's life. Most women go through the same thing several times."

"I didn't."

"No, you just had one big tragic heartbreak. I can't imagine how tough that must have been when he was your one and only."

"Is."

"Excuse me?"

"He still is my one and only."

"Oh. Sorry. Anyway, Trev will be fine. He'll recover."

"I hope so. He was so excited about his plans—working construction, volunteering at the station, the house he hopes to build someday."

"And he'll be excited about those things again."

"He's not, now?"

"No, but that's natural. Like I said, he'll be fine, given time."

"How much time?"

He gave her a puzzled glance before returning his attention to the road. "That's hard to say."

The finality in his tone kept her from asking anything else.

Three hours later, he stopped for some fast food and pointed the truck toward Eagles Nest. "You'll have to give me your impression, but I thought everything went great."

"It did go great." She juggled her burger and drink while she made sure he had access to the fries. "Suzanne is exactly the kind of person I was hoping to find. Once she gets some assurances from her colleagues, I'll provide her with more details."

"She seemed fine with that."

"I think she understands the stakes and why I'm being careful. She acted like she didn't want too much info at this stage, in case she slipped up and gave something away."

"Exactly."

"Thank you, Zane. I couldn't have done this without you. She obviously trusts you and that gave me credibility."

"We've been working together on the raptors for a while. She's quite the fan of those birds. She's promised to find me a low-cost source for ghillie suits."

"I heard her mention that! What the heck are they?"

"They're hooded camouflage suits that keep you from looking like a human when you feed a baby raptor. You don't want them thinking humans provide food."

"So you look like a big bird?"

He laughed. "More like a Dementor from the Harry Potter movies, but it seems to work."

"I can't wait to see one, now. What great work you're doing."

"Thanks." He sighed. "But we lost a bald eagle on Monday. She flew into a windshield and then was hit by another car. We couldn't save her."

"Oh, no! Do you know if she had babies?"

"Not sure, but they'd be out of the nest by now, so that helps."

"What about her mate?"

"He'll mourn for a while, maybe a couple of years. Then he'll find a new mate."

"I thought bald eagles mated for life."

"They do, assuming they're both alive. But their lifespan is around thirty years in the wild. If a mate dies, mourning for years would be a waste of breeding time. Nature doesn't work that way."

"Huh. Are there any animals that mourn for the rest of their lives?"

"I'm no expert on this, but I think there's only one. Us."

"I thought there were others. Another myth exploded." She finished her burger and wadded up the wrapping before stuffing it in the bag. "More fries?"

"No, thanks." He handed her his balled-up wrapper. "You can drop this in the bag and ditch the rest of the fries if you don't want them."

"Okay." She rolled up the bag and shoved it beside her seat. She was busy digesting the info about eagles choosing a new mate a couple of years after their mate dies when Zane broke the silence.

"I'm poking my nose in, but I have to ask you something."

"What's that?"

"Why are you so concerned about Trevor?"

Her pulse jacked up. "Because I like him. We're friends."

"That's it?"

"Well, yeah. I don't like to think of him being sad. He deserves to be happy. He's a great guy. I mean, he was the one who climbed to my roof a million times during the fire to put out any hotspots. And the reroofing job, where he'd only let me pay for the materials, that was amazing."

"Then there's going down in the cave when he was terrified."

"I know." She swallowed a lump of misery. "I hate thinking of what he went through on Sunday, poor guy. When he got to the bottom he was so shaky. I just...I was hurting for him. But he had to do it. Stubborn, crazy, wonderful man that he is."

"Hm."

"What?"

"I wish I'd taped that."

"So he could hear it? That wouldn't help."

"No, so you could hear it."

"Why?"

"You sound like a woman in love."

"I do not." She folded her arms over her chest.

"I've talked to him, Olivia. He doesn't expect you to stop loving Edward. He only wishes you'd start loving him. He thinks you don't. I think he's wrong."

She groaned and flopped back against the seat. "That's not love. It's just—"

"Here's the deal. If you'll open your mind to the possibility of loving Edward for what you had then and loving Trevor for what you have now, I'd be eternally grateful." He glanced at her. "And we'd be even in the favor department."

"You drive a hard bargain, Zane McGavin."

"I'm a Scotsman. I know how."

* * *

Although Zane hadn't taped her words so she could play them back, he might as well have because she couldn't forget any of them. Or any of Zane's words. She couldn't forget the bald eagles, either. No doubt Zane had told her that story on purpose.

Most of all she couldn't forget Trevor, a man she missed more desperately with every passing day. On Saturday afternoon, she climbed into the cave, sat on her favorite rock and told Edward what was in her heart. Then she climbed out again. Now she needed to tell Trevor.

She texted him, and when he didn't reply in thirty minutes, she checked with the fire station. He wasn't on duty. Next she called Kendra.

"He's at the GG. Do you want me to—"

"That's okay. I'll track him down. Thanks." Dear God, was he drowning his sorrows? Zane had said he was rough around the edges. Did that mean he was spending his free time getting drunk?

She drove there berating herself for causing him such anguish that he had to numb it with booze. It was a little past five when she walked in and the band had just started. Customers filled most of the tables.

She couldn't find him at any of them. What if he'd left? She hurried over to the bar where Bryce was mixing drinks. "Where's Trevor?"

"Hey, Olivia. He's in the back getting more napkins."

"Why is he doing that?"

"Mike needed time off. He's taking an online course in business management and needs to study for a final next week. Luckily Trevor was available to help me tend bar."

"So he's working? He's not getting…" She gulped as he came out of the kitchen. He didn't look drunk. He looked gorgeous. He'd worn that same shirt the first night they'd made love.

He stopped when he saw her. At first his eyes lit with eagerness. Then his expression closed down. He went behind the bar and opened the package of napkins. "Hey, Olivia." He didn't look at her. "Just stopping by?"

"No, I came to see you."

"Bad timing. I'm not exactly available right now." He stacked napkins in the holders all along the bar.

"I see that." She was to blame for the way he was behaving. She squashed down her impatience and did her best to sound reasonable. "When will you be available?"

"No telling. Probably best if you text me."

"I tried. You didn't answer."

"Probably didn't hear it. Gets loud at the GG."

She pulled out her phone. "I'm texting you right now."

"I'll look when I get a chance. I have to check on a dinner order." He pushed through the swinging doors into the kitchen.

Bryce finished making two salt-rimmed margaritas and placed them on a tray that the server whisked away. He gave her a sympathetic glance. "Sorry, Olivia. He's hurting pretty bad."

"I know." She typed her message in all caps and hit Send. Then she waited. She was counting on his curiosity to get the best of him.

Evidently it had, because he charged out of the kitchen and left the doors swinging wildly behind him. He came toward her, his chest heaving. "You do?"

She nodded.

"But what about..."

She closed the short distance but didn't touch him yet. "I will always love him. Just like I will always love you."

He let out a whoop of joy and pulled her into his arms. "Hey, Bryce, she loves me! She loves both of us!"

"She loves me, too? Hey, I know we're twins, but—"

"Not you. Her late husband. Never mind." Trevor gazed into her eyes. "I love you so much. I—"

"Trev, hate to bother you," Bryce said, "but orders are piling up."

She smiled up at Trevor. "And you love your brother, who needs you right now."

"Yeah, he does, but—"

"Go tend bar. I'll sit on a stool the whole night and keep you company. It's the least I can do after what I've put you through."

"It could be a long night."

"I'll wait for you."

"Sit down at the end by the kitchen. Then I can come around and kiss you whenever it gets slow."

"I can do that."

"But here's one to get you started." He laid his hat on the bar and dipped his head. "I love you, Olivia."

"I love you right back, Trevor."

His kiss was sweet and gentle at first but soon became hot enough to bring catcalls and applause. At last he lifted his head. "There's more where that came from."

"That's why I'm here. I want all the love I can get."

"I hope you're prepared, 'cause you're gonna be up to your eyeballs in love." He tucked the phone with her message in his shirt pocket, right over his heart.

She gave him a smile so big it made her cheeks hurt. "Can't wait."

It's Christmas with the McGavins for former Air Force pilot Badger Calhoun, but an unexpected encounter with Hayley Bennett lands him in the role of pretend boyfriend to help her avoid her mother's holiday matchmaking schemes in A COWBOY'S CHRISTMAS, book six in the McGavin Brothers series!

* * * * *

Hayley's mom gave her a quick hug. "Oh, honey, he's perfect."

"He is?" Hayley caught herself. "I mean, yes, he certainly is."

"The minute I saw him I knew he was right for you." Her mom took dessert plates out of the cupboard and set them on the counter. "But I never dreamed he'd be the perfect son-in-law for your father. He's going to love having Badger in the family."

"Mom, we're almost engaged, but it's a little early to toss around terms like son-in-law."

"You'll be engaged before this vacation is over. I saw the look in his eye."

"You did?"

"That man's crazy about you." She took a pumpkin pie and a can of whipped cream out of the refrigerator. "Would you please switch on the coffee? It's ready to go." She took a knife out of the wooden block on the counter. "I just wish I could call him Thaddeus. It's so much more elegant."

"But he hates the name." Hayley turned on the coffee pot and took mugs down from the cabinet above it.

"How can he? He's named after his father and grandfather!"

Hayley had considered that, too, especially after finding out that he'd chosen Eagles Nest over Atlanta for his first stateside Christmas. But she wasn't willing to share her speculations with her mother. "Maybe he was teased in school."

"I suppose he could have been. Kids will do that." Her mom sliced the pie. "But I love that kind of tradition. I wanted to name Luke after your father but he wouldn't hear of it. He's never been overly fond of his name, either. I guess I should be grateful he doesn't want to be called Raccoon or Porcupine."

"I like Badger. It's—"

"Did I hear my name mentioned?" The man in question appeared in the kitchen doorway.

She looked over at him. Sure enough, he was standing smack dab under the mistletoe. Her mother always hung it there to go with her holiday apron that said *Kiss the Cook.* "I was just saying to Mom that I like your nickname."

"And I don't *dislike* it," her mother said. "But I think your given name has a certain ring to it. I hope you're planning to use it on the wedding invitations."

Hayley gulped. "Mom, we haven't exactly—"

"Don't worry." He gave her a quick glance. "We'll use it on the invitations."

"Oh, good."

"The pie looks amazin'. I came in to see if I could carry anything in for you."

"That would be lovely." Her mom glanced at him. "Hayley," she said in a sing-song voice. "Look where he's standing."

"What?" He turned right and then left. "Is this a bad place?"

"Oh, no, you're in the exact right place," her mom said. "Go on, Hayley. Claim your kiss."

He looked up and spied the mistletoe. "Aha." Amusement flickered in his eyes as Hayley approached. "Guess I'm caught."

"Seems like it." She couldn't be tentative about this kiss if she wanted her mom to believe they were madly in love. Her heart beat so loud she was scared he could hear it or worse yet, her mom could.

Arms at his sides, he watched her.

"First time under the mistletoe." She slid her palms up his solid chest. The guy had some serious muscles. And surprise, surprise, his heart was going fast, too.

"Then you best make it good, darlin'."

New York Times bestselling author Vicki Lewis Thompson's love affair with cowboys started with the Lone Ranger, continued through Maverick, and took a turn south of the border with Zorro. She views cowboys as the Western version of knights in shining armor, rugged men who value honor, honesty and hard work. Fortunately for her, she lives in the Arizona desert, where broad-shouldered, lean-hipped cowboys abound. Blessed with such an abundance of inspiration, she only hopes that she can do them justice.

For more information about this prolific author, visit her website and sign up for her newsletter. She loves connecting with readers.

VickiLewisThompson.com

Lightning Source UK Ltd.
Milton Keynes UK
UKHW040908190620
365202UK00001B/167